BOOK TWO

History of the West with Sam Payne:
PONY BOY

BOOK TWO

History of the West with Sam Payne:
PONY BOY

CODY ASSMANN

Published by:
Cody Assmann 2021

First Printing: 2021
ISBN:978-1-7375272-1-3

Cody Assmann Publishing
401 East Ave. E
Oshkosh, NE 69154
www.frontierlife.net

Special discounts may be available on quantity purchases by schools, museums, or historical institutions. For details, contact the publisher at the website listed above.

This book is dedicated to those who make a living in the saddle.

INTRODUCTION

Physical geography was one of the greatest challenges America faced as it sought to expand its borders from the Atlantic to the Pacific Ocean. In a world of planes, trains, automobiles, and two-day shipping, we can forget just how big America really is. In total land area, the modern United States takes in over 3 million square miles of territory. This makes America the world's fourth largest country. Our physical geography is not always welcoming either. America is home to lofty mountain ranges, swollen rivers, and large deserts. Today, we pass over these obstacles with relative ease. Our only concerns are that we don't blow a tire, run out of gas, or lose cell-phone coverage. Boy, we've got it rough.

Although faced with months of privation and potentially life-threatening travel, by the mid-1840s pioneers were traveling in waves across the continent. Bound for Oregon and California, by the tens of thousands they cut deep ruts in the dusty Oregon Trail. As more and more people moved, more and more people were motivated to take the risk and make the journey as well. By 1860, there were around 390,000 people living in California and Oregon, as well as over 100,000 others scattered throughout the Great Plains, Rocky Mountains, Southwest, and Great Basin. As people moved, cities grew, governments were established, and new states were added to the Union. Despite the fact its pioneers had overcome geography to move west, the vast distance between east and west still plagued the country.

One problem was the movement of goods from the manufacturing centers in the east, to the frontier towns of the west. If you read *And the Wagons Rolled,* you realize armies of bullwhackers and muleskinners helped overcome this challenge. In addition to the movement of goods, there was the additional challenge of moving people and information. There were also political challenges taking place. You might remember learning about a series of pre-Civil War compromises that preceded the secession of Confederate states. In history classes, those compromises are generally used as an example of how the United States was steadily growing further and further apart on the issue of slavery. Sometimes we forget the real challenges statehood brought. Take California for example.

California became a state in 1850. As a state, it was entitled to representatives in both the House of Representatives and the Senate in Washington D.C. Traveling by land, it would take those representatives as long as 8 months if they traveled overland. By sea, the time could be cut

II

to perhaps 4 months. Either way, those are serious journeys, so it's likely they would not be frequently traveling back and forth. Secondly, any information regarding political decisions would take a similarly long time to reach the citizens of California. It's not hard to imagine that by the time Californians were first hearing about a political situation, the law might already be written. By 1860, there was a serious demand for a service that could better provide correspondence between the east and the west. The result was the famed Pony Express.

The Pony Express was a mail service created by the company Majors, Russell, & Waddell. Already a titan of freighting, they were the likely choice to undertake the daunting task of linking the country with a fast mail service. Luckily for them, they had an example to follow. In 1858, John Butterfield had opened a mail service that traveled from Tipton, Missouri, to San Francisco, California. He named his business the Butterfield Overland Mail service. The Butterfield route dropped south out of Missouri, crossed Arkansas, Texas, and New Mexico Territory, before swinging back north through Los Angeles on its way to San Francisco. In his first attempt, Butterfield delivered mail from west to east in 24 days and 18 hours. This was quite an achievement.

Although Butterfield had accomplished quite a feat, Russell, Majors, & Waddell, thought they could do better. To achieve this, they were determined to follow a more direct route. Instead of swinging south like the Butterfield route, Russell, Majors, and Waddell used then west to Carson City, then over the mountains to Sacramento.

Preparing the line was a massive undertaking. It required an investment in building stations, hiring men to operate them, finding riders, and, of course, buying horses. By 1860, the Pony Express was open for business, and it began taking correspondences from St. Joseph, Missouri, to Sacramento, California. The company met their goal in besting the Butterfield route, and they were generally able to deliver mail in just 10 days. This was nearly instant communication in 1860. For all that it accomplished, it's no wonder the Pony Express has gone down as an epic in Western history.

Of course, the riders have garnered their fair share of attention. Called "Pony Boys," riders were generally small, young men, who had a lust for adventure and fast horses. Riders typically carried the mail between "home" stations roughly 60 to 70 miles apart. These home stations were where the riders slept, ate, and passed the time between mail runs. In between the home stations, there were also "swing" stations. These were the stations where the riders briefly stopped, changed horses, swapped the mail, and maybe took a drink of water before bounding down the line. Riders generally kept their horses in a lope, and traveled at around 12 miles per hour. Although this may not sound fast, it takes serious effort to stay in the saddle at that pace. Buffalo Bill once said, *"fifteen miles an hour on horseback will in short time shake any man all to pieces."* Riders like Johnny Fry, William Campbell, and "Pony" Bob Haslam thrived under these conditions, and they became legendary in their own time. However daring the riders were, it seems necessary to say a word about the horses as well.

Often overlooked, the horses of the Pony Express were the motor of the mail service. It was only through their coiled muscles, elastic tendons, beating hearts, and massive lungs that the mail could be delivered. Through wind, rain, sleet, and night, the unnamed Pony Express horses dutifully, though perhaps disgruntledly at times, ferried the fabled riders across the sandy western landscape. Alexander Majors, part owner of Majors, Russell, & Waddell, wrote, *"The horses were mostly half-breed California mustangs, as alert and energetic as their riders, and their part in the service – sure-footed and fleet – was invaluable."* Russell strikes a chord of truth here, perhaps beyond his intention, when he describes the horse as *"invaluable."*

On foot, a man was helpless in the West. On the back of a horse, he was transformed. No matter the ethnicity, race, age, or physical prowess, people of all kinds capitalized on the gifts horses provide. Whether it was a wandering trapper of the Rocky Mountains, a raiding Comanche warrior, or a cowboy riding drag, without the horse, their way of life in the 19th century would have been impossible. The land was simply too big, and too dry, to be traveled efficiently on foot. It was a fact every plainsman was well aware of, and one that Sam Payne is forced to learn in this book.

Pony Boy finds Sam Payne stationed as a stock tender in a desolate Pony Express station known as Mud Springs. While the Pony Express riders receive all of the glory, they were not the only people that made the mail run smoothly. Station keepers managed each station along the way. Larger stations also had stock tenders to keep the animals ready for their runs. Although Sam has higher aspirations, like many inexperienced youths, he finds himself doing a monotonous job in a monotonous place. However, he keeps his eyes open, and when he gets an opportunity to carry the mail he is quick to strike. His story quickly takes an unexpected turn, and he is forced to realize his own shortcomings and how dependent he is on the anonymous horses he rides.

Although the Pony Express has gone down in legend, the truth is that it did not operate as a mail service for a very long time. Financially, the venture was sinking like a rock in water. There were simply too many expenses and too few mail articles to stay profitable. The business was also competing with the birth of a new technology that would make communication nearly instantaneous; the telegraph. By October of 1861, the first transcontinental telegraph line was complete and the Pony Express was in its final days. The enterprise was simply drawing too heavily on the company to continue, the new technology was unbeatable. In October 1861, the Pony Express made its final ride.

Even though the Pony Express only lasted around 18 months, you could argue that it has been rightly remembered. Not only did it link the nation and achieve its goals, but it served as an example of just what the young country might achieve if it set its mind to a task. It was the answer to the seemingly insurmountable challenge of overcoming the physical geography that plagued America during the 19th century. Rather than rely on their own abilities to overcome their geographic challenges, the operators of the Pony Express turned to one of human's most trusted companions, and valuable helpers. It was in fact, the tandem of man and horse that made the settlement of the west, as we know it, possible.

Enjoy the read, and thank you for your support.

Cody Assmann
August, 2021

HOW TO USE THIS BOOK

First off, I'd like to say a very sincere "thank you" for taking the time to read this book. I've tried to make this book different from any other book I have seen. The book is filled with questions, activities, and video extensions. Given there is so much crammed into these pages, you might find yourself wondering how to best use this book.

The short answer to that question is to use the book however you see fit. Even if you simply read through the book from start to finish and skip all of the added material, you should gain a better understanding of the time period. Although this is true, the quickest way to advance your understanding is to answer the questions at the end of each chapter. Each chapter contains recall questions from the content as well as higher-level-thinking questions that do not have cut-and-dry answers. You'll need to use your thinking skills on those.

For the activities, I would encourage you to do as many as you have time for. How better to understand the life of a mountain man than to live in his moccasins for a few days? Scanning the QR codes in the book, or searching keywords on frontierlife.net, will take you to videos and blogs about how to complete projects, or learn more about frontier life.

If you are a teacher, this book was definitely written with you and your students in mind. My hope is you can use it to meet the needs of your high-ability learners within the regular class time. Assign your students to read the book, answer the questions, and do as many activities as time permits. Of course, if you have alternative assignments that fit better with your curriculum, be sure to substitute those for the activities found in the book.

If you have any questions or comments, feel free to contact me at my website, frontierlife.net. Enjoy!

FRONTIER SPEAK

For the first time reader, this list of phrases and terms might be helpful to understand the lingo of the frontier.

Beeves	Plural for beef cattle.
Buffler	Buffalo.
Cannon Bone	Large leg bone of a horse that is below the knee and above the fetlock.
Cap	Percussion cap used to ignite a black powder gun.
Chips	Dried cow, horse, or buffalo manure used for fire fuel.
Coon	A friendly term used by mountain men.
Flea-Bitten Gray	A horse or mule with a white undercoat spotted with small dark gray dots all over its body.
Forage Cap	A soft cap, usually having a stiff brim, which made up part of a soldier's uniform.
Fresh	An energetic and unworked animal.
Gelding	A castrated male horse.
Ground-Hitch	To drop the reins to the ground and have the horse stand as if tied.
Jug Head	Referring to a horse that has a long-rectangular head.
Lariat	A rope used as a lasso.
Lost my Hair	Been scalped.

Mealy-Mouthed	A dark horse or mule that has a pale color around the mouth.
Plug	A bite of tobacco off a larger portion.
Quirt	A short-handled riding whip.
Rawhide	Untreated animal skin.
Sand	Toughness.
Shanks	The sidepiece of a bit. The longer the shank, the more leverage the rider has on the horse's mouth.
Sutler	A person who sells provisions to army soldiers.
Tenderfoot	An inexperienced man on the plains.
Yarnin	Telling stories.

HISTORY OF THE WEST WITH SAM PAYNE

CHAPTER 1

Dust fogged the corral so thickly, Sam could see only the dim outline of the big-chestnut <u>gelding</u> he was battling. The <u>rawhide</u> <u>lariat</u> in his hand pulled tight as the horse made another attempt to escape. Feeling the power of the horse about to overwhelm him, Sam tightened his grip.

You ain't gonna get the best of me, he thought.

Although properly raised in Leek, England, young Sam Payne had already picked up the talk of the American plainsmen. "Ain't," "gonna"; these were just a few of the words that would have caused his mother to frown. Still, she might be pleased to learn he hadn't picked up the habit of cussing like the other men did. Not yet, anyway.

1

At only 16 years of age, Sam's adoption of the plainsman's habits was born out of necessity more than anything. Life in the West wasn't a picnic. Right now, he was battling a high-spirited horse that outweighed him by over a thousand pounds. The two were locked in a struggle, and Sam wasn't about to give an inch. Determined to win, he dug the heels of his black knee-high boots into the fine dust of the corral. It hadn't rained in several weeks, and the dust was powder dry. The more the horse and man fought, the more the choking dust filled the air and amplified the chaotic scene.

As the horse made its dash, Sam sat back against the lariat. In doing so, the lariat tightened down around the horse's neck, cutting off some of its air. As it felt the pressure around its neck, the chestnut lunged forward in an attempt to break free of the threatening feeling. Overmatched as he was, Sam was incapable of holding back the powerful horse. The rawhide rope slid through his tight grip as the horse skittishly bolted away. A hot-searing pain flared in his palms. Sam let out a quick cry and instinctively loosened his grip. Feeling a release of the pressure, the chestnut charged to the other end of the corral to gain as much distance as it could from the man. In its wake, the rawhide rope danced and bounced off the dirt as it trailed along. Finding itself trapped in another corner, the gelding pranced nervously and lifted its head over the top rail, seeking escape in the prairie beyond.

"What's the hold up, Sam?" came the shout from the station keeper.

Normally quick to answer the call of duty, Sam instead looked down at the bright pink burns crossing his palms. His bare flesh glistened in the mid-day sun. Although not serious, the burns felt like hundreds of tiny fire ants were tearing at his skin. Sam tried to shrug off the pain. He vigorously shook his hands, somehow hoping that doing so would shake the pain away.

It didn't.

"I said, Sam, what's the hold up? Willy will be here this morning with the mail. Henry's horse has to be ready."

Mostly concerned about his burning hands, Sam turned to the station keeper and replied, "Yes, sir, Mr. McArdle. I'll get him ready."

Despite his call for urgency, James McArdle just stood-by and watched him. He had apparently witnessed the tussle from the doorway of the sod-walled building called Mud Springs Station. Unwilling to let Sam admit defeat, the short Irishman felt the need to spur him on. Having forgotten to don his black, wide-brimmed hat, McArdle's bald and sunburned head shone like an apple in the hot August sun. Instead of lending a hand though, McArdle just shielded his eyes with one hand while he watched Sam work in the corral. Sam had worked for the Irishman long enough to know that McArdle believed in a few things. Those things included being on time, keeping Mud Springs clean, and letting the stock tenders deal with the horses. Currently, the other young stock tenders were off gathering chips for the cooking. That left Sam to do the wrangling for rider Henry Wright's upcoming departure. Trying to flex away the still-stinging pain, Sam turned back to the chestnut.

The big horse was still looking for any avenue of escape. Carefully, Sam worked his way toward the nervous horse. Having grown up as a stable boy in England, Sam knew horses and was cautious around them. He constantly kept his eyes moving. A touchy horse was dangerous, and many a man had taken his last breath just before a flashing hoof crushed his skull. As a boy, Sam remembered seeing the corpse of one man whose head had been caved in. It was not the type of thing a person forgot. In spite of the danger, over time Sam had grown accustomed to the unpredictability. Risk was just part of life working with horses, and working with horses was what he had hired on the Pony Express to do.

Initially, Sam had come looking for work after finishing a freighting trip from Nebraska City to Denver City in the spring of 1860. During that trip, he'd seen a few Pony Express riders galloping over the dusty road. Just the sight of those dashing riders had fostered in him a deep yearning to be one of them. After the freighting trip was over, he'd gotten a note from the wagon boss named Dutch recommending him for work on the Pony. Luckily for Sam, he'd hired on a freighting outfit operated by the company Majors, Russell, and Waddell. It just so happened that Majors, Russell, and Waddell also operated the Pony Express. It hadn't taken much to convince station keeper Joseph Moss at Julesburg to hire Sam. Sam remembered Moss had read the note from Dutch, then looked at him and nodded. "You're hired," he had said.

Sam's heart had raced. Getting a job with the Pony had been much easier than he'd expected. He had half-expected to have to demonstrate his riding skills or otherwise showcase his horsemanship. Instead, he just showed the note and got the job. To his dismay, it didn't take long for the other shoe to drop.

Moss had tucked the note away and continued speaking, "We need another stock tender up at Mud Springs. It's a full day's ride from here. You can take your mule and follow the next stagecoach when it goes that way. Shouldn't be more than a day or two."

Sam tried not to let his disappointment show. He'd hoped to be a rider, not a stable boy again. His whole childhood had been caring for horses. Now, he was ready to be the rider, not the caretaker. Without showing his dissatisfaction, Sam nodded and accepted the job. It wasn't the job he had wanted, but Sam knew too much about hunger and poverty to turn down a paying job. Having run away from the protective walls of his childhood home, Sam didn't have many misconceptions about what it took to stay alive. After first landing in New Orleans, he had come close to nearly starving to death on those city streets. The memory was too fresh to risk going through that again. No matter what it took, he was determined to build himself a life out West.

Back in the corral, Sam had snuck close to the tail of the lariat that was lying in the dirt. Stretched out like a snake in the dust, it was almost close enough to grab. Looking the situation over, Sam made a quick plan. He hoped he could grab the end of the lariat and wrap it around one of the posts before the horse bolted again.

"Easy there," Sam said softly.

Wide-eyed, the nervous horse was still hunting a hole in the corner.

Bits of rocks crunched under Sam's boot as he moved a step closer.

With the lariat finally in reach, Sam down bent slowly and made sure to keep one eye on the horse.

"It's alright, boy," he said soothingly.

Reaching down, he picked the last few feet of the lariat out of the dust. Now, if he could just wrap it around an upright post.

He took a step toward the fence. The trailing lariat moved in the dirt and bumped the chestnut's hip. The touch shifted the horse's attention from escape, back toward the rope and Sam. Just the slight touch had caused the horse to tense. Sam knew it would bolt at any moment.

Don't make him blow, Sam reminded himself.

Ever so gently, Sam threaded the tail of the lariat between the rails. The chestnut eyed him warily. Although the horses were all broke to ride, some had never been handled much and were nasty when working around them on the ground. Sam figured the chestnut was maybe five years old. It was old enough to know the routine but still young enough to have some fight. Sam figured he'd win the battle, but it wouldn't be easy. Working snorty horses from the ground was always harder than working from their back. On the back of a horse, Sam figured he could go wherever it went. On the ground, however, he was at a disadvantage.

"Easy, boy," Sam repeated as he threaded more of the rope around the upright.

Slowly, he passed more rope around, and soon, he had a full wrap around the cedar post. As he pulled the last of the slack through, the rawhide made a buzzing noise as it scraped the wooden rail. The slight noise was just enough to set the horse off. It sprang down the fence to flee the danger. In the same instant, Sam tightened his grip on the lariat. He had managed to secure his hold just as the horse hit the end of the lariat. The rawhide stretched tight but didn't snap from the force. Instead, the horse ran in a half-circle through the corral like a fish on a line. Sam knew he had it.

"Now I got you," he muttered as he wiped his rope-burned hands on his dusty pants.

Vocabulary:
Gelding – A castrated male horse.
Lariat – A rope used as a lasso.
Rawhide – Untreated animal skin.
Chips – Dried cow, horse, or buffalo manure used for fire fuel.

Extension Content:
Access the QR code or search "Mud Springs" at frontierlife.net to learn more about the western Nebraska Pony Express station.

Primary Source Extension:
The following description comes from Edward Burton's book *The City of the Saints and Across the Rocky Mountains* that describes his 1860 adventure. Here he describes two stock tenders catching mules for a stagecoach.

"Then two men entering with lassos or lariats, thongs of flexible plaited or twisted hide, and provided with an iron ring at one end to form the noose the best are made of hemp, Russian, not Manilla-proceeded, in a great "muss" on a small scale, to secure their victims. The lasso in their hands was by no means the "unerring necklace" which the Mexican vaquéro has taught it to be: they often missed their aim, or caught the wrong animal."

Primary Source Follow Up:
1. How does Burton describe the lariat?
2. How does Burton describe the men's skill with the lariat?
3. Does this surprise you? Why or why not?

CHAPTER 2

James McArdle paced anxiously in the dusty yard between the station and the corral. Dressed in black pants, a white shirt, and a black vest, he looked more like a mercantile man than a station keeper. Sam knew McArdle's pacing was only his way of dealing with nervousness that the horse may not be saddled in time. Working for the Pony Express was all about time. If the business were to make true its promise that it could deliver mail from St. Joseph, Missouri to Sacramento, California in less than 10 days, everything had to flow smoothly across the mail line. That kind of speed wasn't an accident. The riders' duty was to push their horses between stations. The station keepers' duty was to manage the stations. Sam's duty was to make sure riders had a fresh horse saddled and waiting when they rode in. Russell, Majors, and Waddell only allocated two minutes for riders to change mounts at each station. Any delay would reflect badly on McArdle's ability to run on time, and James McArdle didn't intend to for that to happen. Mud Springs was always early.

Sam pulled the chestnut across the corral toward the stable. Though still nervous, the big horse had enough experience to know when to give up the fight. As they crossed the corral, McArdle was there to meet them at the gate. Caught up in his own anxiety, the station keeper hurriedly opened it for Sam and the chestnut.

"Come on, Sam. Come on, now. He'll be here any minute," he said anxiously. McArdle's bushy red mustache and equally untamed eyebrows animated his speech as they arched and twitched when he spoke.

"Yes, sir," Sam replied as he led the gelding through. Just as the horse was moving through the opening, the two other stock tenders rounded the corner of the station with a load of chips. Their sudden appearance startled the skittish horse, and it bolted to one side. Sam pulled on the lariat, but the big horse pulled him several steps away from the gate. The gelding was just beginning to stop its feet when Sam heard another voice shout across the yard.

"Hey, Sam! If you need a hand, alls you got to do is ask."

He turned to see Henry Wright standing in the doorway of the station. Henry was about five feet six inches tall, couldn't have weighed 120 pounds, and was just a mere three years older than Sam. That being said, Wright carried himself with a confidence that belied his small stature and commanded a deference. His back was arrow straight, his shoulders were pinned back like a cavalryman's, and he always carried his head high. There was another thing about

9

Henry that Sam admired; he always looked you in the eye. Sam knew the confident rider was testing him, and he knew better than to ask for help. Any man who asked for help fell a few notches in Henry's mind. Sam had no intention of doing that.

"I can get him," Sam called back as he returned his attention to the gelding. He could plainly see the whites of the horse's eyes, and it again looked like it might bolt. Sam felt a rise in his own anger toward the horse for making him look bad. He jerked on the lariat, hoping some stern punishment would remind the horse of its manners. Instead, the horse tossed its head all the more and tried to retreat. It took a few more yanks before the horse finally stopped its feet.

"He looks a little <u>fresh</u>," Henry said, sauntering across the yard.

"I expect he is," Sam replied. "We've been shoveling oats to him."

"That's alright," Henry replied. "I'll get that out of him after the first mile or so. By the time we get to the Court House Station, he'll be so played out he'll have forgot what fresh feels like."

Sam knew Henry was right. Courthouse Station was the next station north. It was named for Courthouse Rock, the rock formation that loomed above it. All of the chestnut's extra energy would surely be spent by the time it loped the 11 miles there. Henry would make sure of that. With the chestnut exhausted, Henry would swap it out for a new, fresh horse to get him to the next <u>swing station</u>. He'd repeat this process a few times before reaching the next <u>home station</u>, nearly 70 miles down the road.

Eventually, the gelding quieted some and allowed Sam to lead it again. Sam was hopeful his bracing of the horse would draw some respect from the rider. Instead of respect, only a slight smirk was on Henry's face.

"You know, Sam," he said confidently, "you don't need to be so gentle with them horses. A big horse like this, it wouldn't hurt him to get throwed and stretched a time or two, to learn some respect."

Henry had been looking at the horse as he talked. Now he turned his attention to Sam.

"You give him to me, and I'll straighten him out."

The look in his eyes revealed that Henry would indeed straighten him out. Henry had earned a reputation for being able to handle the baddest and meanest horses around. He was a fearless rider who could straddle anything with hair and would ride through hell without even slowing down. Bold and daring, he was the type of rider the Pony Express wanted. However, he had also earned a reputation as a man who was hard on horses. When asked about the mean streak, he often gave the same response, "Well, it's a tough land."

At times, Sam cursed himself for not being more like Henry. Deep down, he did feel a little intimidated by the chestnut. It was always a battle with these big horses. Overmatched in every way, Sam had to constantly battle to get his job done. Maybe Henry was right; maybe he did need to get a little mean once in a while.

"I bet you would," Sam replied. "I think I got him settled though. I'll get him saddled for you."

"You best hurry," Henry replied, looking past Sam.

Turning to look over his shoulder, Sam could see a thin trail of dust rising from over the hill to the south. While it could signal many things, Sam had a feeling it would be the inbound mail rider. McArdle had also seen the trace of dust and was now waving his hands and shuffling toward Sam.

"He's comin' now, Sam! Get that horse ready. We'll have to work fast to make the change in time!"

Motivated by the rising dust in the distance, Sam pulled on the lariat to lead the horse into the stable.

"And, Sam," Henry said as he walked past. "Grab that bit with the long <u>shanks</u>. He might need it."

"Sure thing," Sam replied.

The familiar dank smell of the stable filled Sam's nose as they entered the sod structure. Earlier that year, when Sam had first seen a sod house at Dobytown, he had laughed at the oddity of a dirt building. Now, he appreciated the cool temperature within the sod buildings. Although the morning sun outside was already making him sweat, the cool air inside the soddy was refreshing.

He led the horse to the nearest stall and tied it securely. Sam quickly removed some debris stuck in the animal's hair. If these were under the blanket when the horse was saddled, they could cause a sore to form quickly. A sore horse was a slow horse, and they couldn't afford that on the mail run. Next, Sam threw on the blanket, followed by the saddle. He pulled the cinch snug and grabbed a bridle off the wall. He had several to choose from but selected the bit with the long shanks like Henry requested. The shanks gave the rider more leverage on the mouth of the horse, and it could be painful if used harshly. Sensing Henry's mood, Sam almost thought about hanging it back up and selecting a bit with less shank. Instead, he walked over to the chestnut and slipped the long-shanked bit in its mouth. Henry wanted the long shanks, and that was what Sam would give him.

Leading the horse back out of the dingy stable, Sam squinted his eyes as he looked south. The trail of dust had gotten much closer, and now the figure of an incoming rider was easy to see on the large flat to the south and east. In the yard, Henry was strapping on his spurs and readying for his ride. He stood erect as the stock tender named Luke brought him a holster with his Navy pistol tucked in it. Wright pulled out the revolver and checked to ensure each of the cylinders had a <u>cap</u> and was ready for use. Satisfied, he returned the pistol back to its holster and looked toward the oncoming rider.

Walking across the yard, Sam felt a familiar feeling of envy bubble up inside him. Sam had been doing the hard work all morning. He had hauled water from the spring, caught the horses, done the saddling, and then done all the other chores McArdle ordered. Although thankful for a job, the work could get monotonous. Then he saw Henry standing in the yard. Dressed in tall-black boots, loose-fitting brown pants, a red-flannel shirt fluttering in the breeze, a rawhide <u>quirt</u> on his wrist, revolver on his hip, and a wide-brimmed, cream-colored hat on his head, Henry Wright just *looked* like a Pony Express rider. The only adventurous thing about Sam was the Bowie knife he kept on his belt. Even more vexing, was the fact that while Sam would soon be shoveling horse manure, Henry would be dashing at high speed across the prairie, delivering mail destined for California. Sam sighed. Maybe, some day, he'd catch a break.

Now, the rider was swinging around the low hill directly south of the station. In just a few seconds, he'd be in the yard. All the hands at Mud Springs were waiting in anticipation.

Henry turned and looked at Sam, who was now standing beside him with the chestnut. He had a determined look in his eyes when he spoke. "You got him cinched up tight?"

Sam nodded. "He's ready to go."

"Good. He's about to get a lesson he won't soon forget."

13

The rhythmic drumming of hooves was now mixed with the labored breathing of the incoming horse. On its back was a small rider named Willy Palmer. Willy was riding a big-black horse, and Sam could see sweat lathered all over it. Horses were always played out when they showed up, and Sam knew the chestnut would look the same when it reached Court House Station. As Willy came dashing into the yard, he pulled on the reins, and the horse instantly skidded to a stop.

Without wasting a second, the sweaty rider swung out of the saddle and pulled the leather mochila off in a single motion. The mochila was a leather contraption that contained the mail in four locked pockets. The company had designed the mochila to fit over the top of all their saddles. This not only allowed for quick changing of the mail, but also ensured the mail would not be lost unless the rider was thrown. Tossing the mochila to Henry, Willy smiled as he shouted, "Here you go, Henry! She's all yours!"

Henry snatched the mochila out of the air and slipped it over his own saddle. All the commotion caused the chestnut to prance nervously. In spite of this, Henry grabbed the saddle horn, stepped in the near stirrup, and vaulted onto its back. Once mounted, he roughly pulled on the reins and turned the horse around.

"Thanks, Willy! See you on the turnaround!"

Having said his good-bye, Henry roughly pulled the chestnut back around to facing west and then spurred the gelding harshly. Finally free, the big chestnut sprang out of the yard like a mountain lion had leapt onto its back. Letting the horse run, Henry freely applied the quirt as the duo dashed away. All morning that gelding had wanted to run, and now, Henry was going to make it pay for that.

Given two minutes to make the change, the Mud Springs crew had made their change in less than one. Before the full two minutes had passed, Henry Wright and the skittish chestnut were already crossing over a rise to the northwest out of sight.

Vocabulary:
<u>Fresh</u> – An energetic and unworked animal.
<u>Swing Station</u> – A station on the Pony Express mail line where riders carrying the mail switched horses.
<u>Home Station</u> – A station on the Pony Express mail line where riders slept and rested between mail runs.
<u>Shanks</u> – The sidepiece of a bit. The longer the shank, the more leverage and control the rider has on a horse's mouth.
<u>Cap</u> – Percussion cap used to ignite a black powder gun.
<u>Quirt</u> – A short-handled riding whip.

Questions:
1. What was the pouch called that the riders carried?
2. How did the mail change horses when the riders switched?
3. Like Henry Wright, most Pony Express riders were small. Sources say the company wouldn't hire men over 120 pounds. Why do you think that was its policy?

Extension Content:
Access the QR code below, or search "How the Pony Express Worked" at frontierlife.net to learn more about how the Pony Express was able to move mail so quickly across the country.

Research Extension:
Here is a picture of a mochila drawn by frontiersman and early western historian William Henry Jackson. As you can see, the mochila draped over the saddle and would be simply moved from one saddle to another to speed up the mail change.

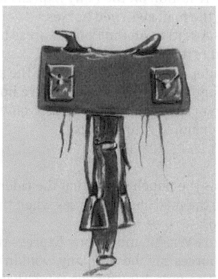

CHAPTER 3

After Henry had ridden away, the work around Mud
Springs didn't stop. Willy's hard-ridden horse needed to be
unsaddled and rubbed down. Afterwards, it could be turned
out with the other horses to graze the already cropped-close
grass around the station. Sam was a little disappointed that it
was Luke's turn to mount up and keep them close. The job of
wrangling the horses rotated between Sam, Luke, and the
other stock tender named Daniel Van Housen. It was a job
each of the young men enjoyed because it was one of the few
jobs done from the back of the mule. Sure, wrangling could
grow monotonous at times, but it sure beat hauling chips,
fixing tack, cleaning stables, or whatever else McArdle bossed

17

them to do. On the back of the mule, at least Sam could imagine he was riding with the mail.

Other than the Pony Express, overland travelers using the road also frequented Mud Springs. Every year, tens of thousands of people used the roads throughout the West to travel in their search for opportunity. Some traveled on stagecoach, some were families with covered wagons, other were freighters, and still others were simply riding horseback. On the road between Julesburg and Fort Laramie, the one thing all travelers had in common was that they all needed water. With few sources to pick from, everybody stopped at the muddy spring that was just a stone's throw north of the station. Years before it became a Pony Express station, James McArdle had selected Mud Springs for a building site because he believed it would be a good spot for a road ranch. Road ranches had been selling travelers goods, food, and lodging ever since the Trail to Oregon had been established decades ago. McArdle had chosen his location correctly, and the Irishman managed to make a decent living in the dry country.

To say the land around Mud Springs was dry seemed to be an understatement. The fact was that Sam had never believed a land could be so dry. Coming from England, Sam was accustomed to the sea of emerald green that dominated the summer growing season. It was a comforting green, and the grass was soft to lie and walk on. Out in the American prairie, however, it was surely different. When he'd come west in late spring, the land near Julesburg had blushed a faint hint of green, and Sam thought it would be just like home. Instead, after the summer sun had beat down upon it, all the grass had turned a pale yellow. It was brittle to the touch, not at all inviting like the lush green he had known as a boy. At times, the land seemed so desolate that Sam didn't know how anybody, or anything, could go on living here. He got this feeling most when he climbed the ridge to the northwest.

Mud Springs sat on a flat at the bottom of some broken hills. Aside from the constant mosquitos living near the spring, it was not a bad location. It was just big enough to hold the station, the corrals, stables, road, and the spring. To the east, the flat extended into the dry wash, gradually sloping upwards to the crest of a hill about a mile away. To the south, a low set of hills rose quickly, wrapping westward and to the north, becoming a low ridge with a tall washed-out cliff face. The road going north, led travelers up and over the ridge and out of the Mud Springs flat.

While the confining hills down on the flat gave a person a sense of comfort, the view of the country was limited. When he had the chance, Sam often liked to follow the road north and sit on the ridge. From there, Sam could see for miles and miles. Far off to the northwest, he could see two rocky bluffs rising out of the prairie. These were Courthouse Rock and Jail Rock. He'd never been to those rocks, but Sam knew that was where the next station was. Between here and there, the land lay sprawled out like a dull-yellow blanket beneath the seemingly endless blue sky above. Far to the north, white sands of the great desert shone like a bleached bone in the sun. Sam didn't know much about that place, only that for forty or fifty miles there was nothing but a barren wasteland north of the North Platte River.

Between his little ridge and those barren hills, Sam knew there had to be maybe twenty miles separating them. What struck him most was the fact that oftentimes there was not a solitary sign of life in the entire expanse. Occasionally, he would see a herd of buffalo. They were usually far off and much closer to the water of Pumpkin Creek or the North Platte River. Antelope were about the only animal that came near, and they were mighty few. Other than that, it was a great big nothing. Sam couldn't tell why he liked it.

Back at the station, Sam once again found himself shoveling horse manure out of the stable and corral. Hot as it was, McArdle demanded the horse manure be removed on a daily basis. It wasn't as much about keeping the smell pleasant as it was about keeping the flies away. Mud Springs usually had only three or four horses on hand at any time. Still, even just a few horses could pile up manure in a hurry. According to his orders, Sam had to take each shovelful 50 paces away from the corral and spring. The boss was particular about that.

Sam took his time hauling the manure away. After all, it wasn't the worst job at Mud Springs. He'd been lucky to avoid the chip-gathering job. Besides, the chips around the station were growing thin. Before long, they might even have to rig up a sled with a basket to start carrying them back. While there was a work mule, it didn't take long for somebody to find use for it. Other than the mule, they didn't use much animal power. McArdle was against using horses for any task other than riding the mail. The company's orders were to have the horses in top shape for their runs. That meant lots of time grazing, oats, and little to no other work.

Although still young, Sam was beginning to question the company's thinking. Partly, that was due to Henry's opinion on the subject. "Horses are for working," the confident-young rider had often said. In his way of thinking, without people caring for them, those horses would have a lot harder time surviving. Oats delivered from Julesburg helped keep them fat and energetic, while men around the station kept the skulking wolves away.

"Heck," Henry had once said, "much as we take care of 'em, these boys ought not to nary lift a finger when it comes to work."

McArdle had been unwilling to give in to the younger man's way of thinking.

"No," he responded with a discouraging shake of the head. "The horses are for carrying the mail."

Then he turned with a twinkle in his green eyes and said, "You'll want a fresh horse if the Indians get after you, Henry."

"Ha!" came Henry's mocking laugh. "Them Injuns want to catch Henry Wright, they'll have to contend with his friend, Mr. Colt." With that, he gave a smug smile and patted the butt of the Navy revolver on his hip.

The confident gesture had done nothing to persuade the stubborn Irishman, who only shook his head. "At Mud Springs, the horses carry the mail. That is that."

As Sam cast a shovel full of manure across the tinder-dry prairie grass, he wondered if Henry had been right. Here he was sweating to haul away the horses' manure so flies wouldn't bother them, and McArdle wouldn't even allow him to rig up a sled to a horse so as to haul it out in one load. It would only take ten minutes, and then, the horses could go back out and graze. Maybe these horses ought to do a little more work around the place.

Before turning back, Sam took a moment to take off his hat and wipe the sweat off his brow. He knew he ought not to complain. Not only would that put him in bad standing with McArdle, but if the haughty Irishman hadn't listened to Henry, he certainly wouldn't listen to Sam. Taking a deep breath, Sam put his hat back on his head and plodded back to the stable for another shovelful of horse poop.

Just another day at Mud Springs, he grumbled to himself.

Questions:
1. What geographic features caused the Pony Express to build a station at Mud Springs?
2. How many horses were kept at each station at a time?
3. Why do you think they didn't keep more?

Extension Content:
Access the QR code below, or search "Black Powder Revolvers" on frontierlife.net to learn more about the revolvers Pony Express riders carried.

CHAPTER 4

Days at Mud Springs passed as monotonously as the turning of a waterwheel. Each morning, all the horses needed to be grained and have their feet checked. McArdle was adamant about this daily routine. Grain kept them running, and a bad hoof would lame one between stations. These chores generally fell to Sam. Although he felt a swell of pride for being noted as competent in the matter, dealing with the high-energy horses wasn't an easy task. Some were hard to catch, and most generally fought him while he checked their feet. Unwilling to surrender, Sam fought back just as hard as he could. He knew enough tricks that he always got their feet checked sooner or later.

After that, the horses were turned out to graze. Every few days, it was Sam's turn to ride the mule and keep the animals grazing within eyesight of the station. On the other days, he hung around, and old McArdle never had a problem keeping his hands busy.

Willy, who was generally game to help, had taken sick with fever the day he had ridden in. Chills had overcome him, and the normally able man could hardly move from bed. Sam could tell he was darn sure sick. There wasn't much anybody could do except bring him water when he asked. Even if they wanted to help, the nearest doctor was at Fort Laramie, more than 100 miles away. Sam figured Willy would mend; it'd just take some time.

As much as anything, Sam was disappointed at the absence of Willy's company. Willy was a fun man to be around. He had stories, jokes, and had a way of talking that made a body like him being around. Even if he didn't help much with the chores, at least he would stand by and entertain while the work was getting done. Whether it was stories from his brief experience on the frontier or his dreams and aspirations for the future, Willy was a talker.

"You know, Sam," he would often say while Sam was involved in some menial task, "I think I might like to head down to Texas some day."

Then he would stare off as if visualizing the image in his mind.

"Yep," he'd continue, "I've heard one man say they got good cattle down in Texas. With as many people as there are heading West, a man selling beef would do mighty well. Once this secession talk dies down, I might just have to head south and see if I can't get my hands on a few <u>beeves</u>, and bring 'em up here to the Platte somewheres."

Then he'd grin at Sam, "And you're coming with me, right, Payne?"

Normally too busy for dreaming, Sam would just continue with his job and reply, "Sure, Willy. I'll go with you."

Aside from Willy's stories, columns of dust rising from the prairie were the only indication things at the station might get exciting. By August, trail traffic had slowed considerably, as most folks traveled west in the spring and summer months. Still, there was a fairly steady stream of people that passed through. One coach even brought a man that had come clear from England. When he'd heard the news, Sam was excited at the prospect of talking with a man from his own mother country. However, it didn't take long for Sam to decide against it. The man did nothing but complain about the weather, the coach, the food, and anything else that he could. He even managed to complain about the antelope steak they served him for supper. Although Mud Springs wasn't fancy by any stretch of the imagination, the man's complaining insulted them all.

Folks out west didn't have much, but they didn't complain about much either. It was a difficult life away from civilization. That difficulty either built a man up to where he could stand on his own two feet, or it tore him down and he died or left. The folks that stayed appreciated an antelope steak even if it was tough. Sam had eaten enough boiled flour to know that steak of any texture was a treat. Heck, it was better than wolf steak. Oddly, Sam felt a distance toward this man who less than a year ago would have been a fellow countryman. Instead of introducing himself, Sam just kept his distance until the man departed the next morning.

Not long after he left, Sam was out shoveling horse manure when he saw a trail of dust rising in the north.

Might be Henry. That'd be a day early though.

25

Still, that sort of thing wasn't out of the ordinary.

"Better get one of the horses caught," he mumbled aloud.

Sam turned, hollered, and waved to Daniel Van Housen who was sitting rigidly on the black mule. Dan, as they called him, had been watching the herd intently. Dan was a good worker but was as single-minded as anybody Sam had ever known. Sam's call roused Dan out of his trance, and he looked to the north. Once aware of the incoming rider, Dan used the mule to herd the horses back toward the corral. For his part, Sam went to the stable and grabbed a handful of oats. Jogging back to the corral, he sprinkled the oats into the trough that stood in the center. The grain made a little sprinkling sound when it hit the wood. At the sound, the horses pricked their ears and came in on a trot. McArdle hated wasting oats, but he also hated to be late for a switch.

As the last horse came in, Sam swung the gate closed behind them. Dan trotted the mule up and stopped by the gate.

"Who do you 'zink it is?" he asked Sam in his heavy German accent.

"Not sure," Sam replied. "But I thought it'd be good to have the horses ready if it's Henry."

McArdle was walking across the yard toward them. His brow was deeply furrowed as he squinted toward the dust. Once again, his bald head was shining in the sun. Why the man even owned a hat, Sam had no idea.

"Willy is not fit to ride," the station keeper said. "He's still sick with fever this mornin'."

His face was flush red with frustration. It was plain to see the problem was weighing on McArdle. "I guess Henry will have to carry the mail to Julesburg," he said, unhappy about the thought.

26

The idea wasn't unheard of. A few stories had come over the trail that riders occasionally made back-to-back runs. It was hard on the men, but Pony riders weren't made of butter; they were hard-riding, adventure-loving men. Most of them would only smile at such a challenge. Sam figured that's what Henry would do. If the column of dust were Henry, the lean rider would have already ridden fifty miles since early this morning. He'd be dusty, hungry, and tired, but Sam figured he'd slap the mochila on a new horse and dash away over the horizon.

Soon, the column of dust was directly behind the northern ridge. It took a little longer than expected, but eventually the form of horse and rider crested the skyline. It looked like Henry, but something seemed off. He wasn't galloping fast in his normal fashion. He had the horse running in a swinging lope that he kept all the way into the yard. Although Sam couldn't put his finger on it, something just seemed odd about the way Henry was riding. It looked like he had a leg just hanging off. By the time he had ridden into the yard, Sam could see the grimace on his face and knew something wasn't right.

"What's the matter, Henry?" McArdle asked in his thick Irish brogue.

"This brain-dead horse fell over on me," Henry said in disgust. At the thought of it, his anger flared, and he pulled hard on one rein to spin the lathered horse into a tight circle.

"You alright?" Sam asked.

"Made it here, didn't I?"

The stinging retort was followed by a momentary silence.

"Well, don't just stand there, Payne, grab my horse, so I can get off this cussed thing," Henry snapped.

27

Not wanting to provoke Henry's anger any further, Sam stepped over and grabbed the reins. The bay gelding shied its head as if any movement was about to cause pain.

"What happened, Henry?" McArdle asked as Henry gingerly got off the horse.

"Oh, this horse got it in its head it wouldn't cross Pumpkin Crick. I stuck him pretty good with my spurs to make him go. Instead of jumping over, he shied to the side. I jerked on a rein to bring him back, and when I did, he stepped in some mud. Stupid horse slipped and fell over. Happened so fast I didn't have time to jump off. He landed on my leg pretty hard. I was able to stay on when he got back up, but my ankle is awful swollen. I don't think it's broke, but it's darn sure hurt. I'm glad I got a few days to rest up."

An unspoken look of alarm passed between the three station men. It took a second, but Henry realized something was wrong.

"What?" Henry asked. "What's wrong?"

McArdle used the back of his shirtsleeve to wipe away the sheen of sweat that had accumulated on his forehead. "Willy is sick, Henry. He won't be making the ride to Julesburg. We was sort of countin' on you to take the mail."

A contemptuous laugh burst out of Henry.

"Ha! I ain't going," he shook his head. "Not on this ankle, I ain't."

It was easy to see McArdle's mind racing for a solution. Willy couldn't ride. Henry wouldn't ride. He certainly wasn't going to ride.

"I'll do it."

The words jumped out of Sam's mouth before he could stop them.

McArdle turned toward Sam.

"You, Sam?" He asked. "You think you can haul the mail to Julesburg, aye? It's nearly 60 miles, ya' know."

Sam's heart was beating quickly. He'd been over the trail before, but not by himself. However, here was the chance he'd been waiting for. It was the chance to be a Pony Express rider. He couldn't hold back the smile that crossed his lips.

"Yeah, boss, I can carry the mail."

Vocabulary:
Beeves – Plural for beef cattle.

Primary Source Extension:
Read the following primary source from Edward Burton who traveled the Pony Express route in 1860.

"The mountain men are all agreed upon one thing, namely, that the meat is by no means bad; most of them have tried "wolf-mutton" in hard times, and may expect to do so again...

"It is a hard life, setting aside the chance of death-no less than three murders have been committed by the Indians during this year — the work is severe; the diet is sometimes reduced to wolf-mutton, or a little boiled wheat and rye, and the drink to brackish water; a pound of tea comes occasionally, but the droughty souls are always "out" of whisky and tobacco."

Primary Source Follow Up:
1. Do you get the feeling Burton has tried "wolf-mutton"?
2. What hardships did Burton identify that Pony Express stations faced?
3. How does realizing "wolf-mutton" was eaten on the frontier add to your understanding of the time?

CHAPTER 5

After volunteering, Sam quickly moved into the corral with his lariat to catch one of the horses. A raw-boned, flea-bitten gray gelding turned its head when the gate shut. Sam figured it was as good a choice as any. Swinging the lariat overhead, he cast it toward the gray, hoping to make the catch. Although he almost missed, the rope came down over the horse's head. As expected, once the gray felt the rope squeeze around its neck, it quickly darted away from the pressure. Sam had anticipated the move and was already countering the pull with his own weight. Unlike the chestnut, the gray pulled for a moment but then gave into the pull of the lariat. After exiting the corral, Sam took it into the stable, saddled it, bridled it, strapped on some spurs, and within ten minutes, was ready to go.

Exiting the stable, Sam led the gelding toward Dan who still held Henry's horse. As Sam approached, he saw a look of envy in Dan's eyes.

"Are you 'veady for 'dis, Sam?" Dan asked.

A grin spread across Sam's face, "Yep, Dan. I'm ready. I been waiting for this for a long time."

Grabbing the mochila, Sam tossed it on his saddle and prepared to mount. His excitement was reaching a boiling point as he swung into the saddle. After finding his seat, Sam gathered the reins in his hands and was ready to depart. The gray already knew what was about to come and pranced anxiously in the dusty yard. A few minutes earlier, McArdle had ordered Luke to get Sam's revolver from the station. Sam's old wagon boss named Dutch had given him the revolver when Sam had left the freighting outfit. Dutch had said it was company policy that every man received a Bible and a revolver. Presently, Luke handed the gun to Sam in the saddle. Sam nodded as he tucked the gun into his belt. Armed with a Bowie knife, revolver, and a fast horse, Sam felt nearly invincible.

Just as he was ready to leave, the station manager had walked over and laid a hand on Sam's thigh.

"Keep to the trail, Sam, and you should steer clear of trouble."

Sam was hardly listening. He could feel the energetic horse under him tensing.

"And don't run that horse too hard. Save him if you can, aye. Henry said rumor is that Indians been around. You keep an eye peeled. If they make a run at you, just keep that horse a-runnin'."

Sam looked down and saw the worry in McArdle's expression. Hoping to ease his mind, Sam just smiled back.

"Any Indians will have to deal with Mr. Colt," Sam said.

McArdle was not impressed. Instead, he replied, "Just run, Sam."

Just run?

Sam shook the thought from his mind. Why was he so down-and-out? He was ready for the trail. It was what he'd been waiting for. Feeling as confident as he ever had, Sam smiled and called out to Dan.

"See you on the turnaround, Dan!"

With that, he kicked the horse in the sides and put slack in the reins. Ready for the signal, the gray gelding drove off its powerful hindquarters. The initial burst of speed rocked Sam back a little, but he quickly straightened himself and found his seat. Full of energy, the gray shot down the road pointed east and followed the curve as it veered south.

Feeling the rush of the wind on his face, the rippling of the horse's body, and the rush of blood through his own veins, the excitement was too much for the young rider. It had taken months of hard work and some luck, but now he was careening across the prairie on the back of a fast horse carrying mail bound for St. Joseph. Unable to extinguish the feeling boiling up, Sam let out an uncharacteristic shout as he dashed away from Mud Springs.

"Yeeeeehoooooooooo!"

The initial euphoria lasted for the first few miles. After that, both the gray gelding and Sam settled into the rhythm of the road. That rhythm was a swinging lope Sam thought he could sit all day. Sam smiled when he realized that was exactly what he'd have to do.

The country surrounding them changed significantly after the first few miles. Near Mud Springs, there were hills, tall escarpments, and some fairly deep canyons. After the road climbed over the southern ridge, however, it revealed a large sweeping plain. It sloped downhill gently toward Lodgepole Creek twenty-five miles away. Initially, he could see cedar trees on the broken hills to the west. Eventually, those fell away until Sam was surrounded by nothing but grass in all directions.

The first swing station to the south was Midway, nearly 12 miles away. Henry had often bragged about how fast he'd been able to make his rides. Being his first ride, Sam had no intention of running a slow leg. He'd gotten his chance to prove himself, and he was going to make the best of it. As a result, he made sure to prod the big gray whenever it offered to lag. Ever since he'd been at Mud Springs, Sam had been graining this horse, checking its feet, and shoveling its manure. Now, it was the gray's turn to take care of him.

By the time they had covered 11 miles, the gelding was showing signs of wear. Several hundred yards ahead, Sam could see the first station on the otherwise lonesome grassland. With the station in sight, Sam wanted to impress the station keeper. Henry always came running in on lathered horses, and Sam would do the same. Although the gray was worn out, Sam prodded it a little faster. In the yard, Sam saw the station keeper holding a smaller bay horse saddled and ready. After dashing into the yard at a gallop, Sam pulled back hard on the reins. Ready to stop, the exhausted gray stumbled to a stop at the first signal from its rider.

Sam knew he had made good time on the ride. Stepping from the saddle, he was hot and sweaty but eager to start the next leg. Smiling, Sam lifted the mochila off the saddle and led the tired gray to the station keeper.

33

The station man had a long black and white beard that grew to almost his belt. Dressed in plain clothes, dirty from weeks of work, the older man spit a stream of tobacco on the ground in greeting. The overconfident grin faded from Sam's face.

"Run that horse pretty hard," the man said in a gravely voice. Sam realized it wasn't a question.

"Yes, I did," Sam replied. The old man was apparently not impressed with Sam's fast pace. "I wanted to make good time."

The old man worked the plug in his jaw, then spat again. His eyes were judging, but his mouth never did say the words.

"You need a drink?" He finally asked.

"Sure. I could stand a drink."

The old man motioned with his head to a barrel by the soddy.

"Use the dipper."

Not sure what to do or say next, Sam just handed the man the reins and the mochila. He turned and walked to the barrel. Finding the dipper on a peg, he dipped it into the water and then raised it to his lips. The cool freshness of the water felt good after the exercise of the ride. He didn't have time to rest though. After a quick drink, he walked over to grab his fresh horse.

The old man held one of the reins after Sam jumped on the bay. Wanting to get started to the next station, Sam looked down at him with a questioning look in his eye.

A placid glaze was on the man's face as he spoke. "You best save this horse a little more than the last one, son. You never know when you might be counting on him."

For a moment, the man held the rein as if driving the point home.

34

After a few seconds, he released his grip, and Sam reined the bay south. Like at Mud Springs, he kicked the horse into a gallop toward the next station called Pole Creek Number 3. As the horse bounded off, Sam felt the same rush of the wind, the same surge of the horse, but the excitement of his first switch wasn't what he'd expected. He'd just made as fast of a ride as anybody could hope for. He had expected to gain some appreciation from the station manager. Rather than having been met with a compliment, he felt like he'd been scolded.

Instead of heeding the old man's advice, Sam just gritted his teeth and urged the horse faster down the road.

Vocabulary:
<u>Plug</u> – A bite of tobacco off a larger portion.

Extension Content:
Access the QR code below, or search "Common Horse Colors" at frontierlife.net to learn more about the horses described in this book.

CHAPTER 6

After nearly ten miles of following the gradual descent of the plain, the road dropped off a series of choppy hills. From the top of those hills, Sam could see the small sod station called Pole Creek Number 3 situated near the banks of Lodgepole Creek. The thin creek meandered through the valley, creating a ribbon of lush green that contrasted the dull yellow surrounding it. That lush green looked comforting and inviting, but Sam knew he wouldn't be able to stay long.

Pole Creek Number 3, Pole Creek Number 2, Nine Mile, then Julesburg. The routine at each swing station was identical; the station keepers had a mount ready and waiting for Sam as he rode in with the mail. At a few stations, he afforded himself time for a swallow of water. At others, he quickly changed the mochila, jumped in the saddle, and shot down the road headed east. Sixty miles. Six hours. Five horses. One rider. By the time Julesburg was in sight, Sam was worn out. Still, he felt a swell of pride on that last mile. He'd done it. He'd made his first ride for the Pony Express, and it felt like he'd done it in good time, too.

The final few hundred yards required him to cross the South Platte River. During the arid summer months, the South Platte had dried up considerably. Earlier that year, one spot had been swimming depth on his mule. On his mail ride, however, most of the crossing didn't even wet his horse's <u>cannon bone</u>. Even though it was not deep, the crash of the horse's hooves sprayed water high above his head. Caught in the late afternoon sun, the droplets shimmered like fancy crystals as they rained around him. After six long hours in the saddle, the water showering down on him was a welcome delight. Once across the shallow river, Sam spurred the horse over the southern bank. Finally, he made the short dash to the station on the edge of the little settlement.

He passed the small frontier settlement with little effort. Although the town was well-known, it really wasn't much more than a collection of a few buildings. However, its location at the splitting of the road made it a place most travelers stopped. Some people went south to Denver City and the mining of the Rocky Mountains, while others took the northern branch to places like Fort Laramie, Salt Lake City, and even California. After dodging a few of those travelers in the road, Sam loped the tired horse to the station. A young rider with an eager look on his face was already waiting for him. Pulling his horse to a stop, Sam slid off and grabbed the mochila.

"Where's Willy?" The young man asked.

"Sick," Sam said as he passed the mochila off.

"Bad?"

"Bad enough, I guess."

"Huh," the rider replied as if it was something to think about.

For a second, they just stood in silence, as the man pondered the news. Then he asked, "Well, who are you?"

"Sam Payne." He extended his hand. For all the rush Sam had made getting the mail to Julesburg, this rider didn't seem in a hurry. "I'm one of the stock tenders at Mud Springs. Henry Wright's horse fell with him at Pumpkin Creek, and he couldn't make the ride, so I volunteered."

With honest eyes, the Julesburg rider looked Sam up and down. Whatever he was looking for, Sam must have passed the test. The man eventually extended his hand and clasped Sam's. "I'm Frank Campbell. Pleased to meet ya'."

"And the same," Sam replied as they shook hands.

"Get going, Campbell!" came an irritated shout from behind them.

Sam turned, looked, and saw the man he knew as Joseph Moss exiting the station door.

"Just getting' acquainted, Joe," Frank replied cheerily.

"Folks in Sacramento ain't paying you $5 an ounce to get acquainted. Get on that horse and get moving," Joe replied. The banter had a friendly atmosphere, and Sam could tell it wasn't an uncommon occurrence.

"I'm a gettin'," Frank yielded. After swinging aboard his mount, Frank turned and looked down at Sam. "Thanks, Sam. We'll see you on the turnaround."

With a smile on his face, Frank turned the tall-brown horse east at an easy swinging lope.

"There he goes," Moss said. The station manager was now standing by Sam. They both watched Frank as he loped leisurely down the road. "Worst thing about Frank is that he keeps time like an Indian. Still, he's about as good a rider as we got."

Moss turned his attention to Sam, "Where's Willy?"

"Sick," Sam replied.

"Bad?"

"Bad enough I guess," Sam replied again.

This is getting repetitive.

"Huh," Moss replied. "You're riding then. How's your first run? You look like you did alright."

"It was good. I think I made good time at least," Sam replied.

"By the looks of that horse, I'd say you were trying to," Moss said, examining the horse that was still breathing heavily. "You run into trouble?"

Sam shook his head. "No. No trouble. Just trying to make a good run."

Moss smiled. "Sounds like you did. Good job, Sam. Let's get that horse unsaddled and get you some coffee. Supper's almost ready."

After six hours in the saddle, supper sounded like a fine idea.

Sam passed his reins to the blond stock tender who had come shuffling over. Unaccustomed to being a rider, Sam had almost begun unsaddling and rubbing down the horse himself. After passing the horse off though, Sam hobbled toward the station. He hadn't ridden that many miles all summer, and his sore legs testified to that. Tired and sore, Sam imagined he looked like a sixty year old man as he shuffled to the building. As a stock tender, Sam occasionally had been aggravated that the riders didn't help take care of the horses. Now, he realized the toll that a mail run took on a man's body. He was tired.

Crossing the threshold into the wooden building, Sam cast a glance around. Like Mud Springs, it was a simple structure, but it did have a little more refinement. Just the fact it was built of wood spoke to that. Oddly enough though, the first thing he noticed was how much hotter the wood building was compared to the Mud Springs soddy.

At least the snakes shouldn't be so bad, he reminded himself.

Sam hobbled over to the stove and poured himself a cup of coffee. Moss was working at the stove when he said, "Bread and bacon sound good?"

Sam nodded, "It'll do just fine."

Moss laughed, "I hope so. It's all we got. It's about done, too. How's life at Mud Springs?"

"Oh, we're keeping the mail running," Sam said before he took a swallow of coffee. Having not drank coffee growing up, Sam had quickly adapted the drink as a staple of his diet.

"I reckon. You think Willy will be all right? He's a good rider."

"I suppose. He just come up with a fever."

"Fever, huh? Hope he comes out of it. Ain't much a man can do about it, I guess. Might be comin' a day when there's enough doctors to go around these parts. That won't be for a spell, though. Here, grab a plate and eat up. You look like you could stand a meal."

Sam grabbed himself a tin plate, and he let Moss load it with steaming bacon and a hot piece of bread. Heat from the summer's evening, combined with that of the cook stove, made the inside of the station feel like an oven. Sam decided to take his supper outside. An old wooden crate propped against the outside wall appeared to be serving the purpose of a chair. Sam eased himself down on it and took a seat. It sure felt good to give his legs a break. Appreciating the chance to rest, he looked toward the sunset as he fed a strip of bacon into his mouth. Low in the sky, the sun was a flaming orb of yellow and orange, casting bright rays across the prairie and the dusty road. A wagon entering town creaked from its burden, and the oxen drawing it bellowed in defiance. Somewhere further away, Sam heard a drunken man shouting and cussing. It wasn't as calm as Mud Springs, but it was still a peaceful prairie evening.

Sam took a deep breath. He'd had a long ride, and now, his job was done. In just a few days, he'd have to turn around and make another run over the same country. He imagined it too would be a long run. A satisfied smile spread across his face at the thought.

Just the life of a Pony Express rider.

Vocabulary:
Cannon bone - Large leg bone of a horse that is below the knee and above the fetlock.

Questions:

1. What was the rate to send mail on the Pony Express?
2. Officialdata.org speculates that $1 in 1860 is worth $31.69 in 2021. Calculate the price for shipping 1 ounce of mail on the Pony Express in 2021 dollars. Next, calculate the price for shipping 1 pound of mail with the Pony Express into both 1860 and 2021 dollars.

   a. Author's note: As a result of the high prices, mail shipped using the Pony Express was often small and to the point. According to the National Parks Service, there was also a special paper used that was extremely lightweight. Using this "Pony Express paper," people could send 8 or 10 pages for $2.50 in 1860. Despite this lower cost, the price was too high for just sending letters to loved ones. Most correspondence on the Pony Express was government or business related.

Research Extension:

Access the QR code below or search "Food on the Pony Express" at frontierlife.net to see what a common meal at a Pony Express Station might have looked like.

Primary Source Extension:
Read this entry from Richard Burton's book describing food at
the stations along the Pony Express route:

*"Our breakfast was prepared in the usual prairie style. First the
coffee — three parts burnt beans, which had been duly ground
to a fine powder and exposed to the air, lest the aroma should
prove too strong for us — was placed on the stove to simmer till
every noxious principle was duly extracted from it. Then the
rusty bacon, cut into thick slices, was thrown into the fry-pan:
here the gridiron is unknown, and if known would be little
appreciated, because it wastes the "drippings," which form with
the staff of life a luxurious sop. Thirdly, antelope steak, cut off a
corpse suspended for the benefit of flies outside, was placed to
stew within influence of the bacon's aroma. Lastly came the
bread, which of course should have been "cooked" first. The
meal is kneaded with water and a pinch of salt; the raising is
done by means of a little sour milk, or more generally by the
deleterious yeast-powders of the trade."*

Primary Source Follow-Up:
1. What foods does Burton say were "usual prairie style"?
2. How would you describe his feelings toward the food?
3. What do you think he means when he says, "*antelope
   steak, cut off a corpse suspended for the benefit of flies
   outside, was placed to stew within influence of the
   bacon's aroma.*"?

CHAPTER 7

Sam had a few days to kill before making his run back to Mud Springs. During his stay in Julesburg, there wasn't much to do besides walk through the mercantile, go to the river and sit, or loaf around the station. In the evenings, about the best entertainment was to watch freighters stumble in and out of saloons. The third night, he even got a chance to see two drunks square off in a fistfight. Unfortunately for Sam, the fight ended quickly with neither man having scored a direct hit. One man took a glancing blow to the chin and tipped over on his back. Off balance from the momentum of his swing, the other one spun and fell like a bag of oats into the dust. For a few minutes, both squirmed around before helping each other get to their feet. Propping each other up, the two eventually stumbled their way toward their wagons.

Other than that, there wasn't much to do. It was a lot like Mud Springs in that regard. Sam got so bored, he even helped out with some of the stock tending. Although he didn't help shovel any horse manure, he did help check the horses each day and rub them down. Aside from those few chores, he didn't want to step on anyone's toes and sort of stayed to himself. About the only other thing he could do was plan his next ride. He knew the route, and now, he had some experience. He wanted to make this next ride even faster than his first. Even though much of it would be a gradual climb, Sam thought he could improve his time. It was just before noon when Frank Campbell came carrying the westbound mail. After a few days of sitting around, he was a welcome sight to Sam.

As Frank loped in, Sam could see his horse was sweated up, but not nearly as bad as Sam's had been on the ride in. Instead, both Frank and his horse looked like they could keep going on to Lodgepole if need be. It struck Sam as odd. None of Henry Wright's horses ever came in looking like that. But here was Frank, loping in like he was on his way for a Sunday picnic. Rather than jerk his horse to a stop, Frank gradually slowed it from a lope, to a trot, before a light pull on the reins caused the horse to stop. It all looked different than what Sam was used to.

"Howdy, Sam!" Frank hollered good-naturedly as he stepped from the saddle. "How's Julesburg?"

"I'm ready to ride."

"Ha! I'll bet. I don't much like staying in one spot long neither. Well, here you go," Frank said as he handed the mochila to Sam. With a chuckle, Frank added, "Bound for some rich businessman in Sacramento. Maybe a love letter

45

from his mistress back East. I hope his wife ain't the one that picks up the mail!"

Sam just laughed and shook his head. He knew the mail was mostly business and political, but the thought of it was enough to make him blush. Joking wasn't Sam's strong suit, so instead of playing along he just grabbed the mochila.

Tossing it onto his own saddle, Sam stepped on the sorrel horse he had saddled and was ready to make his run. "See you around, Frank. Thanks for the food, Joe," Sam shouted to the station keeper who had stepped into the yard.

"Any time, Sam. Good luck on your ride. Maybe we'll see you again someday."

Reining hard, Sam put spurs to the sorrel and dashed down the main road before taking the northern fork to cross the river. Within a few minutes he had crossed the shallow river and was once again on dry ground. Back on solid footing, Sam quickly pushed the horse faster. At the rate they were traveling, the sorrel would soon be plumb worn out. It mattered little to Sam, though. He knew there would be another horse waiting for him at Nine Mile Station. All that mattered was time.

The changes were quick at Nine Mile, Pole Creeks 2 and 3, and Midway. As with his previous mail run, each station keeper had a horse ready for him. When Sam dismounted from his hard-ridden horse at Midway Station, the black and gray bearded man again had a disapproving look on his face. He didn't say much this time, though. He just spat a stream of tobacco juice and handed Sam the reins to a fresh bay.

After an hour of loping, the bay horse was beginning to tire from the speed and gradual climb. Sam could see the final ridge in front of him, and he knew it was downhill after that.

"Come on, you lazy thing," Sam urged the horse with voice and spur. "We're almost there."

Weary, the bay horse snorted and angrily tossed its head from the prodding.

"What's your problem?" Sam said in irritation. He, too, was growing tired from the ride. "Get going!"

Along with the angry shout, Sam hooked his spurs into the horse's sides. Rather than submit, the horse pinned its ears and humped its back. Feeling the power of the horse coil beneath him, Sam knew what was coming. In a split second, the bay horse ducked its head and tried to dump its rider by making a few powerful jumps. Luckily, Sam had anticipated the action and squeezed his legs tight. He was a good rider, and the sudden jumping failed to dislodge him from his seat.

Still in the saddle after the horse's best effort, Sam knew he had won the battle.

"Alright, you ready to go now?" he snapped.

Another kick to the ribs signaled the horse it was time to go forward again. Tired from the run and deflated after its sudden burst of energy, the horse snorted in defiance but wearily loped toward the ridge. Sam could see defeat wash over the horse's demeanor. He'd snapped its fighting spirit.

"That'll teach you," Sam said under his breath.

Cresting the ridge, Sam saw a whiff of smoke coming from Mud Springs although he could not yet see the station. Seeing the country around the station was a welcome sight. It'd been another long ride since leaving Julesburg that morning. To add to the miles, the mid-afternoon sun had seemed even hotter than normal. At Mud Springs he hoped to find some shade, a drink of water, something to eat, and some rest. That would suit him just fine.

After loping the horse down the long hill, Sam crossed the flat south of the station. Soon, he could see the tobacco-brown walls of the buildings. Although he expected to see a

47

commotion with his approach, the activity in the yard was totally absent. His first thought was of the mail.

Come on, boys. We can't be late!

As more of the scene was revealed, Sam could see a small group of people clustered at the foot of a hill.

What's going on there?

Keeping the horse at a lope, Sam followed the road past the station and toward the group. The closer he got, the more a knot grew in his stomach. Three people stood in a semi-circle with fresh dirt mounded nearby. Forgetting about the mail, Sam nearly jumped off the horse as he got close. At the disturbance, McArdle turned to face Sam. The station keeper's sunburned face was solemn and ashen.

"What's wrong?" Sam asked nervously.

McArdle sighed deeply.

"Willy is dead, Sam."

CHAPTER 8

"What?" Sam cried. The sudden rush of emotion struck him like a mule kick. "What happened?"

"The fever took him," McArdle replied. "After you left, he got worse and worse. This morning when Luke went to wake him, he was gone."

Dead. Just a few days before, Sam had seen Willy ride in like a hero from a King Arthur legend. He had laughed, joked, and talked about going to Texas. Today, he was gone forever. No Texas cattle. No great adventures. He was in the bottom of a narrow grave. Sam walked over and glanced into the hole. All he could see was a half-worn blanket wrapped around a motionless figure. Beneath those blankets was one

49

of the few friends he had in this world. It was all Sam could do to hold back the flow of tears that suddenly bubbled up.

In fact, he couldn't hold them back.

Turning his head so the others couldn't see, Sam used the dusty sleeve of his shirt to wipe away a trickle of tears. It'd all happened so fast that Sam couldn't make sense of it. Why did something like this have to happen to Willy? He'd never hurt anyone. A million confused thoughts flurried through his mind. No matter which one he tried to grab at, they all ended the same.

It didn't make any sense.

After a minute of letting the raw emotions pour out of him, Sam stifled them as best as he could. Getting himself back together, he turned back to the group. In each of their faces, he could see the same dull and mournful look. Dan was standing quietly with his hands folded as if he were standing in church. His dirty face could not conceal where tears had already cut their course. Henry looked sullen, and all of his color was gone. It looked like Willy's death had taken the wind out of his sails, too. McArdle looked liked he had aged twenty years. His shoulders slumped from an unseen burden that threatened to bury him beneath it. As Sam looked around, an ominous question rose within him.

"Where's Luke?" he asked.

As he had anticipated, a dreaded look passed between the others standing around the grave.

"In bed," McArdle whispered. "He's got the fever, too."

A grim silence hung between them as each contemplated the thought.

"How bad?" Sam asked.

"Bad enough he ain't out here," Henry responded.

The curt reply caused Sam to turn and face the young rider. A bead of sweat glistened on Henry's face, and there was an angry look in his eye. As Sam locked eyes with Henry, he knew something wasn't right. After a second passed, it dawned on him. He cast another observing glance over his friends.

"You're all sick," he said aloud.

Silence affirmed his fear.

After a few seconds McArdle spoke. It wasn't more than a coarse whisper, "Dan says he's feelin' ok."

"Oh, hell," Henry declared. "I'm fit to ride. I could ride to Sacramento and back if I had a mind to."

The look on McArdle's face told Sam the two men had already argued it over, and there was no sense bickering any more.

Looking to Sam, he said flatly, "We need a doctor."

In a moment, the fatigue and exhaustion Sam had felt just a few minutes ago seemed to vanish.

"I can go," Sam without a second thought. "Where do you want me to go?"

"Stand by, kid!" Henry roared. "I'm fit to ride, and I'll be taking the mail with me when I go."

The force in Henry's voice informed Sam all he needed to know about another argument he had missed. Henry was going to try and make his mail run, and there was no use trying to stop him.

"Go get my horse, Dan," Henry gruffly commanded. It was clear that with Willy in the ground, and the mail at Mud Springs, Henry wanted to be gone.

Yielding to the request, Dan scampered off to go fetch the saddled horse.

Silence hung between the three men still clustered around the grave. A mild prairie wind blowing between them served as the only sound. Sam looked at the ground and tried to make sense of the situation. Willy was dead. Luke was sick.

51

McArdle was, too. Henry, who was also sick, was leaving on his mail run. Once he left, it would fall to Sam and Dan to look after the two sick men left behind. He directed another slow glance toward the open grave. Cold fear slowly spread though his body.

Might be me soon.

Sam realized that without medicine, all of them might die from the fever. The unsettling thought caused a haunting feeling to turn his stomach.

Dan brought Henry his horse, disrupting his thoughts.

"Give me the mail, Sam," Henry ordered.

Sliding the mochila off, Sam walked over and handed it to Henry. He took it without a word and slung it over his own saddle. Lacking his normal agility, Henry put a foot in the stirrup and hoisted himself up. Sitting as proudly in the saddle as he could, Henry spoke to the solemn men. "I'll get the mail delivered and bring the doctor. Y'all just hold tight."

"Take care of yourself, Henry," McArdle said, concern on his face.

Henry gave a curt nod, and then reined the bay horse west. "Gidyap!" He shouted as he spurred the horse. Like a shot from a rifle, the horse sprang down the road. Atop the horse, Henry seemed to tip just a bit before catching his balance. Following the bend, before long they had disappeared over the ridge. A dismal hush permeated Mud Springs. Again, the whistling of the wind was the only sound.

After several moments, McArdle walked over to Sam. Anxiously, he grabbed him by the arm.

"You've got to go, too, Sam. Henry won't make it. He's too sick. Saddle up a horse and follow him."

"Where do you want me to go?"

"Nearest doctor is in Fort Laramie. Tell him we've got the fever and ague."

Fever and ague! The thought sent a chill through him. The dreaded disease had killed sporadically throughout the frontier. While working on the steamboat last spring, many of the deck hands had spoken of it with a look of fear in their eyes. Was it the air that caused it? Was it the water? Nobody knew, except that the mysterious disease had killed many. Now, it had killed one of Sam's friends, and it threatened more.

"You sure that's what it is?" Sam asked, hoping for a different response.

The boss shook his head. "I'm not certain, but I feel it in my bones."

Assigned to the task, Sam felt the new burden settle on him. As much as the old station keeper wished to carry it himself, by circumstance he had passed it to Sam. Sick as he was, McArdle simply had no other choice.

Realizing he might be their only chance to survive, Sam nodded his head.

"Ok. Dan, can you catch me a horse?"

Dan still looked scared as he obediently jogged off to go catch another horse. McArdle reached out and took the reins from the bay Sam had ridden in.

"Go get yourself something to eat. You'll need it for the ride."

Nodding his head, Sam walked across the yard on sore legs. Stepping inside, he looked to the cot and saw a bundle of blankets piled over Luke. The sick man moaned and whimpered a little as Sam came in but never came out of his sleep. Trying to keep quiet, Sam crossed the floor, grabbed a tin cup off the wall, and poured himself a cup of coffee. Drinking it quickly, he burned his mouth a little. Still, he knew he would want the rejuvenating effect it would provide. Seeing that morning's bacon in the bottom of a frying pan,

53

Sam grabbed a few slices and put them in his mouth. The burnt meat crumbled in his mouth and mixed with the strong taste of coffee. Taking another look at the sick man on the cot, Sam felt trepidation at his new mission.

All he knew was that Fort Laramie was far to the west. Near as he could tell from the stories, he guessed it had to be over one hundred miles away. Hopefully, Henry would beat him to the next home station at Scott's Bluff and pass the news along. If not, it would be a long ride there and back.

Luke groaned from the blankets again.

"No time to waste then," Sam said to himself as he drank down another swallow of hot coffee.

Extension Research:
Malaria, or fever and ague as it was known on the American frontier, was a deadly disease that many settlers knew. Access this QR code, or search "Fever and Ague" on frontierlife.net, to learn more about this deadly disease.

CHAPTER 9

Dan came out of the stable holding the reins to a small sorrel horse. With so many horses traveling between stations, it was sometimes hard to recognize them. This one, however, had a big blazed face that made it easy to remember. Unlike the thoroughbred horses that dominated the eastern half of the Pony Express, the sorrel was different. It was much smaller, though it still appeared alert and hardy. With its ears pinned and a flash of fire in its eyes, Sam knew it might be a handful.

Dan walked over and handed the reins to him. Sam could see the ever-present flush of red on his friend's cheek was brighter than normal. Silently, he prayed Dan wasn't sick with the fever.

"Henvy alvays said dis von has a deep bottom," Dan stated as an explanation for his choice of horse. "He alvays talked about it."

"Thanks, Dan," Sam replied. "I expect Henry knows what he's talking about."

Without the mochila, Sam checked the pistol in his belt and knew he was ready to ride. McArdle had quickly run inside, and now returned with a small slip of paper in his hand. "Here," he said handing the paper to Sam. "You might need this along the way."

Sam looked down and saw that he had quickly scribbled a note reading:

3 MEN SICK AT MUD SPRINGS. FEAVR AND CHILLS. SUSPACT FEAVR AND AGUE. – JAMES MCARDLE

After reading the note, Sam tucked it into the pocket of his pants. Looking up, he saw McArdle gently petting the sorrel on the neck. Sam couldn't tell if McArdle was trying to soothe the horse or himself. Impatiently, the sorrel stomped a hoof in the dust. Just before Sam put a foot in the stirrup, he quit his fretful petting and turned his attention to Sam.

"Sam, please, save the horse a little, son. We can't afford you to not make it, and you won't make it on a tired horse."

There was a sincere pleading in the anxious-green eyes.

Although Sam had no intention of taking it easy on the sorrel, he didn't want to upset the station keeper.

"Alright, boss. I'll take it easy on him," he said as reassuringly as he could.

Until I get over the hill.

For all they knew, all of them could be dying of the fever before long. So what if a horse got a little tired. Although Sam had tried to put McArdle's mind at ease, the man's worried look never left.

Ready to get started, Sam put one foot in the stirrup and stepped into the saddle. As he did, the sorrel horse pranced nervously. Once seated, Sam cast a glance to the west. One hundred miles away lay his friends' only chance. Hopefully, the news would beat him there with the mail. If not, he knew he had the most difficult ride of his life ahead of him. Before departing, he turned and looked down at Dan and at McArdle. A gust of hot wind blew though the valley and swirled the dust around them. With Willy's grave still open, Luke sick in bed, and McArdle showing signs of fever, Mud Springs was a sad and dreadful place.

"Don't worry, boss," Sam said while trying to act confident, "I'll get through to Fort Laramie if Henry don't."

Without waiting for a reply, Sam turned west and put heels to the sorrel. Rather than move out smooth and straight down the road, the blaze-faced sorrel darted from side to side. It was so sudden and jerky that Sam had trouble staying in the saddle. The horse dodged to the right, and Sam pulled him back to the left. It would follow the pull for a few steps before quickly darting back to the right. Sam pulled hard back again with the same result. The little horse's head was high, and its ears were pricked forward. Sitting in the saddle, Sam could feel it was wound as tight as a spring. Again, the horse darted to the side. It wasn't a promising start to a critical ride.

Sam's anger fanned at the belligerent horse. Forgetting his promise to McArdle, he kicked the sorrel hard. The horse squealed and took a few more running steps forward before bolting to the side again. Every fiber in the sorrel's body was

57

tense, and Sam was busy yanking left and right trying to keep it headed down the road.

At this rate, I'll ride twice the miles to make Court House station, he thought angrily.

Fighting every step of the way, the horse would trot, bust into a lope, then stop suddenly and bolt back the other direction. Unwilling to let it get the upper hand, Sam kept yanking, pulling, and kicking, and eventually the pair had moved over the crest of the ridge. In the distance, Sam could see Courthouse Rock rising above the vast sweeping valley of sunbaked prairie grass. Several miles ahead of him, a trail of dust rose like a column of smoke into the pale blue sky. A speck of a man bobbed at its base. It was easy to see that Henry was riding hard. Mounted on the restless sorrel, Sam knew he'd do nothing but lose ground.

As the road swooped north and down the hill, the sorrel began to loosen up a little. Its head was still high, ears were pricked, and it was blowing hard as if trying to clear out its nostrils. At least the gait had smoothed, and it had decided to follow the road straight. It had tested Sam, and Sam knew he had overcome it.

All right, now let's see how hard you can run. The victorious thought crossed his mind.

Giving the horse some rein, Sam applied his heels once again. With its feet freed up, the horse suddenly busted into a mad dash down the hill. The resulting rush of hot wind over Sam's face nearly snatched the hat off his head. Quickly slapping his hand down to keep it on, Sam could feel the sorrel horse's body ripple as it dashed down the trail. All the pent up energy of the sorrel rushed out as it reached top speed. Sam kept his gaze fixed down the trail that was quickly disappearing beneath him. He barely noticed the yellow blur of grass in his peripheral vision. The exhilaration gave Sam a light feeling as he balanced skillfully in the saddle. A flood of excitement intoxicated him. Since he had come to America, there were few times he had felt this sort of freedom. In that moment, all the worry of the situation at Mud Springs lifted.

As much as it had wanted to run, the sorrel couldn't keep that pace for long. Within a half-mile, it began to lag. At that point, it tried to settle into a smooth lope. Unwillingly to forgive the horse for the delay it had caused, Sam pushed it faster, hoping he could match Henry's pace. As the horse slowed, Sam's mind cleared. Now, he was able to think clearly about his trip and plan. He'd never ridden this way before, but he knew the stations from Henry's stories. First would be Court House Station, then Chimney Rock. Next, was Ficklin's Springs, followed by Scott's Bluff Station. Once he made it that far, Sam knew he'd be able to pass the notice on to a new rider if Henry hadn't already. With any luck, Sam would be making this ride for nothing but precaution.

After Sam had covered half of the distance, he saw Henry's trail of dust vanish. This indicated that he had made the first station at Courthouse Rock. Wanting to keep pace with his fellow rider, Sam kept his horse at the laborious speed. By the time they splashed through Pumpkin Creek, the sorrel was lathered with sweat all over its body. Henry had been right though; the sorrel had a deep bottom and had kept the brutal pace all the way. Also, once the horse had finally lined out, it had traveled as well as any Sam had ever ridden.

Seeing the sod station at the foot of the tall spire, Sam was ready to dismount and begin the next leg of his trip. Still riding hard when he got into the yard, Sam pulled the sorrel to a stop. As he stepped down, a curious man with a bald spot on top of a head that was otherwise covered with unruly brown hair stepped out of the shadow of the soddy.

"Howdy, stranger. What can I do for you," the balding man asked.

"Hi, I'm Sam Payne, and I'm a stock tender at Mud Springs. Everyone's taken sick there, and Mr. McArdle told me to follow Henry with the message in case he don't make it."

A look of understanding appeared on the man's homely face. "I suspected he was feeling poorly. I didn't say nothing to him, though. You know how Henry is. Things bad at Mud Springs?"

Sam nodded, "Pretty bad. Mr. McArdle thinks it's fever and ague."

The station keeper shook his head and mumbled something under his breath before replying, "What is it I can do for you?"

"I'd like a fresh horse."

"Sorry, Sam, I just turned mine out," Sam could hear the disappointment in the man's voice. "I wasn't expecting a change for a few more days. I could try and go catch one, if you'd like. It might take me awhile though. Maybe an hour or so."

Having wrangled horses at Mud Springs, Sam knew it could be faster than that. It also might take longer, depending on the horses. With every passing moment, the sun would slip further and further toward the horizon, and Sam wanted to make as much of the ride in daylight that he could.

Sam figured he'd be better off to try and make the next station on the sorrel. Surely he'd get a change of mounts there. Moving on past the change in circumstance, Sam now understood why McArdle had asked him to save the horse. If something bad should happen, then he'd have a horse still able to travel. Turning to look at the sweating sorrel, Sam could see it was breathing heavily, but its ears were still pricked. Most other horses would have been played out. Sam was grateful Dan had picked the blaze-faced sorrel.

Sam took a swallow of water and walked the horse down to the creek so it could do the same. After allowing it a few drinks, he stepped back into the saddle and turned the horse to the west. With over 12 miles until the next station, Sam realized he ought to go a little easier on the horse this time.

CHAPTER 10

All of the sorrel's excess energy had been burned off on the ride from Mud Springs. Now, instead of dodging back and forth, the blaze-faced horse trotted quietly away from Court House Station. True to its reputation however, its eyes were still sharp, and its ears still pricked. If Sam asked it to travel, the lathered sorrel would continue on. Hopefully, it could keep the pace to the next station.

Keeping in rhythm with the bouncing trot, Sam's eyes surveyed the land around him. He'd never been this far over the trail before, and the view was unexpected. After rounding the foot of Courthouse Rock, the trail swooped over a small ridge and then across an expansive slope that ran toward the

62

river several miles north. Sun-blasted prairie grass grew on the slope like the stubble of a bearded man's face. Only a few shallow gullies and small dry washes broke the flaxen plain south of the river. As the slope leveled off, it met the meandering North Platte River that shimmered and sparkled in the hot-summer sun. Easily over a mile wide, the great waterway dominated the treeless valley. Beyond the northern edge of the river, the land again lifted upwards. The northern horizon terminated shortly at the top of a low rise and appeared sandier than the southern side. Sam recalled stories of a great desert north of the river. This appeared to be the western edge of that great abyss.

Aside from the natural beauty, a wide swath of road cut the prairie on both sides on the river. A straggling freight train trudged through the dust toward their destination. Dwarfed by the immensity of the plain, their white-topped wagons looked like children's toys strung across the valley. It was only from his lofty viewpoint that Sam could truly appreciate how small the impressive freight trains looked in the scope of the world.

Although enchanting, the view of the valley reminded Sam just how small he and his horse were on the landscape as well. After seeing the open expanse, the consequence of what would happen if his horse gave out was very real in his mind. Like it or not, their futures were completely intertwined. If the horse couldn't make it, Sam might not make it. If Sam didn't make it, then what would happen to Luke and McArdle? Pushing the thought from his mind, Sam just focused on making a better ride to Chimney Rock.

Keeping the horse trotting, Sam followed the road to the north and west. Riding at the trot required extra effort from Sam, but he knew it might recuperate his horse a little. Soon, a new wave of sweat was dripping down Sam's body from the work. Ahead of him, Sam could see the column of dust that indicated Henry had gained significant distance on him. He was glad Henry had made the switch at Court House station and hoped he stayed well long enough to carry the mail, and the message, at the standard Pony pace.

For the next few hours, Sam worked hard to stay in cadence with the sorrel. He'd already ridden nearly ninety miles since leaving Julesburg that morning. It was now getting toward evening. Although young and spry, hours of riding had drained the energy in his legs. A dull pain was aching in his lower back. Sores on his thighs, which had been minor irritations in the morning, were now stinging with each painful rise and fall of the horse. He wondered if the combination of sweat, heat, and canvas pants would soon rub a hole clear through his thin legs. Seeing no other option, Sam kept pushing on, mile after mile. As he trotted past the slow-moving freight train, Sam saw the grim determination set in their jaws. It was a reminder that the struggle he faced was not unique. Everyone out west struggled. A body either had to handle it or catch the next stagecoach back east.

By the time he'd passed the freight train, a curious rock formation protruding above the plain stood in plain sight. No one needed to tell Sam it was the famous Chimney Rock. With its tall sandstone spire projecting far above the valley, there was no other landmark Sam had ever seen that could be mistaken for this remarkable feature.

The sight of the rock reminded Sam that the sorrel would soon get its rest. By now, the horse had traveled over twenty miles. It was an honest day's travel on the prairie, and Sam had asked the horse to do it in less than three hours. Resilient, tough, and willing, the blaze-faced sorrel kept trotting toward the descending sun. Already planning the impending switch, Sam intended to keep his next mount fresh longer. There were no promises his next horse would have the same stamina as the sorrel.

With a little over a mile to go, the sun was falling quickly toward the horizon. The sky was a mix of orange, yellows, and reds. Long-dark shadows stretched across the land, creating a contrast of brilliant colors and somber shadows all at once. Across the blazing prairie, a coffee-brown soddy rose humbly from the land. Sam also saw what appeared to be a few riders loping large circles around the structure. Peering into the sun, he squinted to get a better look. At the same time, Sam also thought he heard what sounded like a pop. The noise had been quiet, and when suppressed by the wind, squeak of the saddle, and the heavy breathing of both man and horse, it was almost inaudible. Still, it was enough to perk Sam's attention. Nothing out of the ordinary happened for several seconds until he heard another pop. This time, Sam was sure he heard it. Squinting hard, he looked across the commotion. It now looked like the circling riders were riding fast towards a low rise on the southwest corner of Chimney Rock. What at first looked like a handful of horses, now seemed to have doubled in number. Still trying to make sense of the scene, Sam heard the pop again. His heart nearly stopped.

It was the sound of gunfire.

An ominous feeling rose inside him, and he pulled on the reins to stop his horse. Seconds slowly slipped past as Sam kept close watch on the events and tried to determine what to do next. While he had no desire to ride toward gunfire, he needed desperately to get to the station and get a new horse. In the matter of less than a minute, the men had disappeared, and he decided to cover the last of the distance to the soddy.

By the time Sam got to the station, the scene was quiet except for one man was angrily stomping around the yard.

Now within earshot, Sam could plainly hear the man cussing and shouting in the direction the riders had fled.

It wasn't the man's anger that had Sam on edge as he rode into the yard. It was the fact that Sam didn't see a single horse anywhere nearby.

Apprehensively, Sam rode up to the angry man. "What's the problem?" he asked.

Enraged, the man's face was flushed red as he turned to face him. His eyes flashed, and his voice seasoned with an outrage he didn't try to hide.

"Indians!" He seethed. "Indians just run off with every blasted horse I got!"

Indians!

The thought hit Sam like a ferocious gust of prairie wind.

"You alright?" Sam asked.

Puckering his face in frustration, Sam took the brunt of the man's anger. "Alright? I ain't got no horses! You got any idea what that means for this mail line?"

At that moment, mail was the last thing on Sam's mind.

CHAPTER 11

After letting the sorrel drink, and taking a few swallows of water himself, Sam rode the fatigued horse west out of the station. South of the road was a ridge of rough hills covered in dark green cedars. Had it not been for the circumstances, the rugged hills burning in the setting sun would have been enchanting. As it was, Sam knew the horse thieves could be hiding anywhere in those shadows, watching his every move. Trailed by their own long shadows, Sam and the sorrel jogged toward the next station at Ficklin's Springs twelve more miles distant.

As Sam's tired legs kept rhythm with the clip-clop of the sorrel's hooves, he was doing his best to keep his mind alert. Aside from the fatigue of the trail, the pressure of the message he carried and the shock of losing Willy were all taking their toll. He once again reminded himself that Henry was ahead of him pushing hard. With any luck, he would already be changing out at Ficklin's Springs. That meant the mail and the message were actually traveling much faster than he was. Despite that, Sam felt pressure to keep riding on as if he were the only one Mud Springs depended on.

It didn't take long for the sun to drop over the western edge of the world. After it did, the sky morphed from vibrant reds, yellows, and oranges to subdued shades of blues and purples. Slowly, the darkness of night descended across the prairie. The air cooled, and its soft touch felt good after a hot day in the saddle. The eerie howl of a wolf emanated from the low cedar-covered ridge. In response, several more wolves broke the night with their own hair-raising howls. Although the wolf howls were common on the prairie, hearing the foreboding baying while alone was a different experience. Hopefully, all the dangers lurking south of the trail would decide to stay there. If nothing else, the fearful thought helped to keep Sam's mind alert as dark closed in around him.

By the time he was halfway between the stations, the smothering blackness of a moonless night had fully enveloped the land. As he trotted along, a single dancing flame became visible. Its bright light illuminated the dark prairie like a burning candle.

Must be freighters, Sam figured.

After drawing nearer, Sam knew he'd guessed right. Although the wagons were circled off the road a little ways, Sam reined the sorrel in the direction of camp. If nothing else, hopefully he could get a drink and give the sorrel a chance to catch its breath. There was a chance they'd seen Henry, too.

"Hello the camp," Sam shouted as he drew within shouting distance. He could already see the figures of two-dozen men sitting around the fire.

"Hello," came a gruff shout. "Come on in."

As Sam walked the horse in, several of the men got to their feet and walked out to meet him. One man who appeared to be the wagon boss strode out in front of the rest. He was well built, and his tattered clothes matched the common garb of most freighters. After Sam dismounted, he extended his hand as he walked toward the stranger.

"Evening. Name's Sam Payne."

"Evening, Payne" the man replied. His thick hands squeezed hard as he took Sam's hand in greeting. "I'm Brett Hardy. What can I do for you? You look plumb wore out."

"I'd like some coffee if you got some to spare, sir. I started in Julesburg this morning and been riding hard since noon."

"Julesburg?" came the skeptical reply. "What's the rush? The war start or something?"

Since coming to America, Sam had heard frequent discussion of the possibility of war. He didn't ask much about it, and he figured it was none of his business.

"Not that I know of, sir. I'm with the Pony Express, and I carried the mail from Julesburg to Mud Springs. When I got there, I found out they had taken sick. I'm on my way to Fort Laramie for a doctor."

A mournful feeling welled up in Sam as he thought about young Willy's fresh grave. If he didn't hurry, he feared Luke would soon be buried alongside him.

"Sick?" the man's face soured. "Cholera?" he asked with a hint of uneasiness.

Sam shook his head. "No, sir. The boss thinks it's fever and ague."

69

Realizing he was stalling the rider, Hardy shouted over his shoulder to camp. "Jacob. Bring a cup of coffee to this feller."

Hardy tucked his hands in his belt as he turned his attention back to Sam. "So you're headed to Fort Laramie, then?"

"Yes, sir. The boss says there's a doctor there that might be able to help. He sent me behind the regular mail rider in case something went wrong. You probably seen him this afternoon?"

The look that spread across Hardy's blocky face revealed he had.

"We seen him. Was late afternoon just before we made camp. He come riding by on some snorty black horse. He was slouched in the saddle and white as a cotton bed sheet. We told him he ought to take camp with us, but he groused a little and hardly even slowed down. That horse was givin' him fits, too, and it looked like it was all he could do to just stay in the saddle."

The young man who Sam figured was Jacob came trotting up with a steaming tin cup full of coffee. With a nod of appreciation, Sam took the steaming cup. The first sip nearly scorched his lip, but Sam drank it as quickly as he could. After swallowing down a mouthful, Sam picked up the conversation.

"That was Henry, alright. My boss wasn't sure he'd make it through on account of him being sick, so he sent me."

Brett Hardy shook his head indifferently. "I expect he done right sending you. By the look of him, I doubt he'll make Ficklin's Springs and wouldn't bet a lousy blanket he'll make Scott's Bluff."

As he spoke, Hardy's attention turned to the sorrel horse.

"Speaking of not makin' Ficklin's Springs," Hardy continued. "This horse looks played out."

Sam nodded in acknowledgement. "Group of Indians stole the herd at the last station." The men's ears perked up at the news of horse thieves in the area. "So I ain't been able to switch mounts since Mud Springs. This one's still game though. He sure does got a deep bottom."

"If he made it from Mud Springs this fast, I'd say he sure does," Brett said. He stepped a little closer as if to study the animal. "Not to tell a man his business, Payne, but a man set afoot out here ain't much good a'tall."

"Yes, sir," Sam replied. "I've been trying to save him since Court House Station. With all that's gone wrong, seems more like he's been saving me."

Hardy laughed at the statement. "Yep. A good horse is funny like that."

Sam swallowed down some more coffee as he and Brett talked idly for a few minutes of horses, mules, and cattle. As they talked, all Sam could think about was the image of Henry riding slumped in the saddle in the darkness. With all the dangers lurking about, Sam felt a trace of concern. Hastily, he swallowed down the last of the hot coffee.

"Much appreciated, Brett," Sam said as he handed the tin cup back. "I'll try and repay the favor next time your train comes through Mud Springs."

They shook hands as the wagon boss replied, "Good luck to you, Payne. I hope you make it in time."

Sam's legs had stiffened during the brief rest, and he found getting in the saddle required more effort than normal. Once in the saddle, he said his last good-byes and once again kicked the sorrel into a trot. Night sounds of crickets accompanied the beat of his horse's hooves. After just a few minutes, the flame of the freighter's campfire had dwindled until it disappeared behind a swell in the land. Once again, Sam was all alone on the moonless prairie.

Riding through the dark, Sam tried to keep his imagination in check. It was easy for a man alone to start seeing things in the shadows. Most were likely antelope, coyotes, or other wild animals, but there was also the possibility the shadows were something more sinister. Although he'd come west just a few months ago, Sam had heard enough stories of outlaws, Indians, and other bandits to know the threat was real. Most often, they drifted in and out of the hills near the trail, attacking, stealing, and then retreating back to cover. A solitary traveler such as he was easy pickings. At least he didn't have much worth stealing.

Suddenly, Sam noticed the sorrel prick its ears forward and come alert. Peering through the darkness, Sam thought he saw the faint outline of something moving. A thousand thoughts of what it could be inundated his mind. His blood ran cold and he felt goosebumps tingle on his arm. Pulling the sorrel to a stop, Sam's pulse quickened as he looked and listened. If he had any doubts that something was really out there, all he had to do was look at the sorrel's eyes and ears to realize the shadowy figure ahead of him was not a figment of his imagination.

Several tense seconds past as Sam's mind raced to decide what to do. He couldn't expect to outrun anyone on his tired horse. There was the chance he hadn't been spotted. He might be able to slide past unnoticed. If not, he might be forced to a fight. His hand drifted to the worn handle of the revolver in his belt. A chill went through him at the thought of getting in a gunfight. As his hand contacted the smooth handle, he quietly withdrew the gun for immediate use. Fatigue from the long day had vanished, and now, he was alert and ready.

Quietly he waited, hoping for the apparition to just go away. Then, from the darkness, he thought he heard a muffled sound. Wrestling with his pounding heart and racing mind, Sam tried to calm himself well enough to hear. A few seconds passed, and he heard the sound again. This time he was certain. Cautiously, Sam waited a few more moments. Again, what sounded like a pitiful moaning was clearly audible. Keeping the gun in his hand, Sam gently walked the sorrel toward the sound. The closer he got, the more the dim outline became something real. There was something, or somebody, writhing on the ground. Aware it might be a trap, Sam didn't let his guard down.

"You alright?" Sam asked half-expecting an ambush at the sound of his voice.

The only reply was a loud groan.

Sam nudged the sorrel forward a few more steps. By then, Sam could see the figure of a man curled up into a ball on the dusty road.

"You alright?" Sam asked again.

"Need...help," came the almost whispered reply.

Stepping off the horse, Sam hadn't completely let his guard down as he approached the figure. Kneeling down to get a better look, he tried to roll the man to his back. Sam's heart nearly stopped once he got the man to his back.

It was Henry Wright.

CHAPTER 12

"Henry? What's wrong?" Sam asked.

"Sick," came the mumbled whisper. "Need help."

"Where's your horse?" Sam looked around, desperately.

"Gone...Sidewinder...dumped me."

Gone? That left just one played-out horse between the two men, one of whom was gravely ill, and another who'd traveled more miles since noon than many would travel in a week. With no other options, Sam knew he'd have to walk the rest of the way.

"You can ride mine. How far you reckon it is to Ficklin's Springs?"

Henry moaned painfully as the unseen demon wracked his body. "I...dunno...just....get me...on a horse."

"Alright, Henry. Hold on."

Sam wrapped his arms around Henry and did his best to pull him up to standing. Although Henry's pride prodded him to stand on his own, his body was simply too far-gone to offer much help. It took all his strength just to keep himself standing after Sam had gotten him that far.

Once he was on his feet, Sam ducked under one of Henry's arms and supported him toward the sorrel. Although tired, the sorrel came alert as the shadowy figures stumbled toward it in the darkness.

"Easy, boy," Sam soothed it with a whisper. Luckily, the sorrel stayed put and allowed Sam to grab the rein.

"Alright, Henry, I'm going to try and lift you up there. You think you can manage?"

Although the night was black and the fog of fever was in Henry's eyes, Sam thought he saw a familiar glint of determination in them. Instead of a response, the sick man just nodded his head and closed his eyes as he prepared for the exertion. Sam bent down and wrapped his arms around his friend's waist.

"Alright," Sam said. "Here we go then. One...two... three!"

On three, both men gave their best effort. Sam lifted with all the strength his small and tired body could summon. Henry's hands flailed and luckily managed to grab hold of the saddle horn. With the horn in his hand, Henry pulled and, with Sam's help, he was able to get one foot in the stirrup. After gaining his toehold, both Henry and Sam fought like tomcats to keep his momentum going. With some help, Henry was able to swing his off leg over the cantle. Finally in the seat, Henry found his balance and let out a painful exhale. For a moment, both he and Sam breathed hard from the exertion.

After a catching his breath, Sam asked, "You ready to start, Henry?"

A quiet nod was all Sam got in response.

Grabbing the rein, Sam led the sorrel back to the deeply beaten road and headed west. As they walked in silence, Sam's legs ached and fatigue clung to him like a wet-cotton shirt. Judging by the distance he had already ridden, he didn't think it would be more than three or four miles to Ficklin's Springs. On a good day, that meant maybe an hour of walking. Tonight, he hoped he could make it in less than two. Plodding along, Sam prayed that he wouldn't have any trouble at Ficklin's Springs, and he would finally be able to change horses. He'd pushed the sorrel too hard at first, and now he, the sorrel, and his friends in Mud Springs were paying the price for that mistake.

It took longer than he hoped to reach Ficklin's Springs. Judging by the stars, Sam guessed it had been around three hours since he'd left Chimney Rock. All the while, he'd seen more shadows than he thought possible, and he'd heard more unfamiliar sounds than any time he could remember. Eventually though, the dim outline of a sod structure materialized out of the gloom. Approaching in the dark, Sam figured he ought to shout out and give the station keeper notice.

"Hello the camp," he shouted, not knowing what else to say.

No reply came from the soddy.

Sam led the sorrel into the yard, making sure to make as much noise as possible. Likely being after midnight, he figured the station keeper was asleep. Leading the sorrel to the stable, Sam dropped the reins and ground hitched the horse. As the sound of their steps stopped, Sam listened for some sort of noise.

That's funny, Sam thought. *It's awful quiet.*

True enough, Sam hadn't heard the slightest sound yet. Walking to the stable, he poked his head in to check on the horse that should have been ready for Henry's mail run.

Nothing.

"Surely he's got a horse saddled somewhere," Sam murmured. Walking around the yard, Sam couldn't find a horse saddled anywhere. Then he heard a soft moan escape from Henry who was still in the saddle.

"Just a minute, Henry," he said. "I'll get you down soon."

Again crossing the dark yard, Sam hollered, "Hello! It's Sam Payne and Henry Wright. We ride for the Pony Express. Anybody here?"

Silence.

Approaching the wooden door, Sam knocked gently. "Hello?" he said more softly.

Lifting the latch, Sam swung the door open. Nothing stirred within the black void.

"Hello?" Sam said again. He was as cautious as anyone might be when walking into a dark home with a loaded gun.

Best not to move too fast.

Carefully, Sam poked his head through the door.

Half expecting a shotgun blast to ring out, he was met only with quiet. Quiet except for a rhythmic sound coming from what appeared to be a cot.

Snoring?

"Anybody awake in here?" Sam asked a little louder, hoping to wake the sleeping man up.

No response.

Crossing the threshold, Sam stepped into the stage station. His eyes had adjusted to the darkness, and he could see the station was simple. Two cots, a stove, and a small table, made up the interior. Deliberate with each step, Sam got closer and closer to the cot with the sleeping man. Fortunately, he didn't see a gun anywhere, but he realized a loaded pistol could certainly be under the covers. There was something else on the bed though. Sam's eyes struggled to see what it was.

Another step got him to the bedside.

A large clay jug was tipped carelessly on the cot. From the smell, it was easy to tell it was whiskey. Lifting the jug, Sam could tell that it was almost empty.

Sam's anger flared. It had already been a long day, a long night, and now this. Unable to control himself, Sam dropped the jug, grabbed the bottom of the cot, and jerked it up, shouting, "Wake up!"

The cot, blankets, and drunk man all flipped over and created a tangled mess as they hit the dirt floor. As Sam expected, the man suddenly came alive. Thrashing and shouting curses, he tore at the blankets that apparently bound him. Sam waited until the man had half untwisted himself and rose to his feet.

"Where's my horse?" Sam demanded.

"Who are ya?" the man shouted back.

"Sam Payne, Pony Express rider. Henry Wright is outside. Where's the mail horse?" he shouted angrily.

The man's foggy head ducked as if struck suddenly with the realization of what was happening.

"Oh...well..." he stammered as he closed his eyes against the pain in his head, "I didn't think anybody was due through tonight."

"Well, here I am."

The half-drunk man muttered something under his breath as he continued to untangle himself. It might have been comical, had the situation been different. Try as he might, the man couldn't get free of the blanket twisted around him. Suddenly, his patience vanished, and he shouted and tore violently at his binds for freedom. The result was predictable. Rather than break free, the awkward pressure threw him off balance, and he crashed back into the cot. What sounded like cracking wood accompanied the more general noise of the fall. Deflated, the station keeper momentarily lay on the floor in his fog of drink and confusion.

Fed up with the drunken man, Sam asked directly, "Where are the horses?"

Half-muttering, the man replied, "Horses? Oh...well... Last I seen 'em, they was south of here."

"How far south?"

"I dunno. South."

Sam's anger had not yet died. "How far south?" he shouted.

"I dunno, I said! A little ways."

A little ways? Sam thought. *I might spend half the night looking for them and still not find them.*

"Reckon you can find them?" Sam growled.

"Oh yes, son, I'll find them just as soon as the sun's up. They always come in when I shake that oat bucket."

"Morning ain't good enough," Sam responded. "I got a sick man outside, and sick friends at Mud Springs needin' help, too. My horse has already rode from Mud Springs, and I need a new horse, now!"

"I ain't got one, son. Go rattle that oat bucket and maybe they'll come in."

Sam's anger fumed. Seeing no other choice, he thought he'd just as well go shake the oat bucket a few times and see

79

what happed. "Get up," Sam barked. "I'm bringing Henry in. He's sick."

Angry as he was, Sam felt like delivering the man a swift kick to get him up and moving. Realizing it wouldn't help the situation, he instead turned and stepped back into the night. Walking over to Henry, he reached up to grab the sick man by the waist.

"Come on down, Henry. Let's get you inside."

Sliding off, Henry felt more like a sack of oats than the agile man he was. Combined, their best efforts were barely able to keep him from crashing to the ground. Once Henry found his footing, Sam was able to lead him into the soddy. Inside, the station keeper had finally risen to his feet and was holding his aching head. Sam stepped past him and laid Henry on the other cot. Grabbing the dirty blanket the man had been using, Sam turned and laid it on Henry.

"Get him some water when he needs it," Sam ordered the station keeper. "He's awful sick."

"With what?"

"Fever and ague."

The man unexpectedly perked up. "You think he's got it?"

Sam nodded. "That's what James McArdle thinks."

Nervously, the station keeper looked around. "Can...do you think you can take him to the stable instead?"

"Listen, mister, Henry is stayin' in this cot. Bring him water when he needs it and anything else he wants. If you don't want to hang around, you go sleep in the stable."

With that, Sam walked out, back into the darkness. Head down and hip-shot, the sorrel had not moved since Sam had allowed it to stop. Sam hoped he could still get a new horse caught and leave the sorrel to rest. On the other hand, if the horses didn't come in, Sam would have to ride the sorrel to Scott's Bluff Station. Surely, that would be as far as the horse would ever have to go.

"Let me get you some oats," Sam caught himself saying to the animal. "You've sure enough earned 'em."

Vocabulary:
Ground-Hitch: To drop the reins to the ground and have the horse stand as if tied.

CHAPTER 13

     Standing in the dark, Sam shook the bucket of oats once again. For five minutes after graining the sorrel, he'd shaken that bucket with no results. Apparently, the horses were too far away to hear, sleeping, or untrusting of the sound in the darkness. Whatever the reason, Sam knew they were not coming. Instead, he was left to hold the bucket and contemplate his situation.

     He had heard it was fifteen miles from Ficklin's Springs to the station at Scott's Bluff. 40 miles behind them, Sam figured the sorrel could stand fifteen more. The only other choice was to wait until morning. Thinking about Luke huddled in the cot at Mud Springs, Sam didn't like the idea of wasting the extra time. The sorrel would have to go.

Before getting back in the saddle, Sam checked on Henry in the soddy. He was huddled in the cot, trapped in a fitful sleep. Sam didn't like leaving him with the still-drowsy and drunk station keeper, but he had no other choice.

"Make sure and keep an eye on him. With luck, I'll be back tomorrow from Fort Laramie with some medicine."

Instead of replying, the station keeper groggily waved a hand to signal he'd heard.

Somehow the gesture failed to stir Sam's confidence.

Walking back into the dark, Sam pulled himself back on top of the sorrel. The walk to the station had helped to loosen Sam muscles up, but it had sucked more of his waning strength. Fact was, he wished he could just lay his head down for a few hours. Instead, he gave the horse some rein and gave the signal it was time to move out. Obediently, the sorrel took a few stiff steps before transitioning to a slow and steady trot.

It was an easy gait to sit, and Sam found his mind wander as the sorrel followed the well-beaten road. His thoughts drifted to the loneliness of the prairie that surrounded him. About a mile away from Ficklin's Springs, he passed what appeared to be one of the many graves erected along the side of the road. At times they came in bunches, and at times, they were all alone. Some featured elaborate carving, but most were simple, with a name and a date hastily inscribed. They served as a grim reminder of how quickly life could end out here in the West. Growing up in the city, any corpses were quickly taken away and buried in the cemetery outside of town. Unless a body visited to put flowers on the grave of a relative, the markers weren't seen on a daily basis. That was different on the trail.

This melancholy pondering returned his thoughts back to Willy, Luke, and Henry. Like Sam, all three were young. Each of them had at some length discussed their dreams and ambitions. Although Luke seemed content to tend the stables, Willy and Henry had dreamed some big dreams. Neither gave a thought to tomorrow, aside from the belief that another day would bring them closer to their aspirations. At the present moment, Willy was covered by six feet of fresh dirt. Buried with him was a fun-loving nature, joyful spirit, and friendship Sam had thought he would enjoy for years to come. Worn down from the strain of the last eighteen hours, an overwhelming wave of despair swamped Sam's body.

As the feeling overtook him, he felt vulnerable in the oppressing gloom. He realized there wasn't but a moment between him and the unknown. It might come from an Indian, a bucking horse, or an unseen disease ravaging the trail. Willy hadn't seen it coming. Heck, Henry still didn't see it coming. The realization of how quickly death could come made him feel small and unsure of himself. Instead of being a hard-riding Pony Express rider bravely facing all obstacles, he felt more like a small bug that would quickly be forgotten by the rest of the world. It was a fearsome thought.

Behind the fear, though, a stronger feeling emerged. Sam had been raised in a praying family, and the powerful feeling welling up in him prompted him to send an earnest prayer God's way. Although he might have just been talking to himself, in that moment, he wouldn't have bet on it.

As Sam's mind worked, the sorrel moved along at a ground-eating pace. Suddenly, having seen something it was unsure of in the darkness, the horse shied to the side and almost dumped Sam in the process. Nostril's flared, ears pricked, and muscles tensed, the sorrel quickly broke into a gallop and darted down the trail to make its escape. Having managed to stay in the saddle, Sam just let the sorrel run itself out for a hundred yards or so. After that, although not completely settled, the horse returned to a jogging trot and headed for the shadowy rise of Scott's Bluff that was barely discernable in the distance.

The unexpected incident made Sam appreciate the sorrel all the more. While he himself was contemplating the mysteries of life and death, the sorrel was also living in a world of dangers. Sam didn't know what spooked the horse, and it didn't matter. The sorrel saw something and felt the threat was imminent. Quickly, it had darted away, determined to evade the danger. After a short burst of effort, the animal simply let its fear slide away and returned to life as normal.

As much as he had been taught to doubt the senses of horses, Sam thought in some ways the blaze-faced horse handled its fears better than he had. It didn't go on worrying about what the spook was. It just moved away, got itself safe, and went back to life. Sam let out a deep sigh. Along with it, he seemed to exhale a day's worth of worries as well. Although he hadn't liked the sorrel at first, over the last twelve hours he had grown to appreciate it more and more.

"You're a fine horse, Blazer," Sam said out loud.

Business-like, the newly-named Blazer didn't even break stride.

CHAPTER 14

In a little more than an hour, Blazer had loped and trotted to the foot of the towering shadow Sam knew was Scott's Bluff. Continuing to follow the trail, lofty rock formations loomed like shadowy fortresses on either side. The longer Sam rode, the more these formations funneled closer and closer together. Eventually, the road led to the narrow pass separating the large rocks. Craning his neck to see their tops, Sam could only imagine what they looked like in the daylight. Even at night, they looked impressive.

As soon as he crested the pass, the bluffs quickly receded. In their place was a labyrinth of small washouts and ravines. Slowing Blazer down, Sam wanted to make sure he didn't accidentally take a wrong step and fall to the bottom of one. Although Sam knew the sorrel was sure footed, he also knew it was fatigued and figured it was best just to take his time.

After a few hundred yards, the ravines gave way, and the road swung back to the north. Once the ravines played out, Sam kicked Blazer back into a slow and bobbing trot. After he'd traveled what felt like a mile, Sam saw the dim form of several buildings emerge. In the yard was a stagecoach, and Sam saw the outline of what he suspected was one of the hands preparing the wagon for their day's work. At the sound of Blazer's hooves in the dirt, the man stopped what he was doing and turned his attention Sam's direction.

"Hello," Sam said confidently.

The man waved back and replied "Hello."

"Any body else up?" Sam asked as he eased Blazer to a stop.

"Yessum."

It was then Sam heard the scrap of the door as it opened.

At least they're awake, Sam consoled himself.

"Henry?" A gruff voice broke the night. Although concealed by darkness, the figure in the doorway appeared to be stoutly built with shoulders that looked like those of a blacksmith.

"No, sir," Sam responded. "Sam Payne. I come from Mud Springs, and I'm headed to Fort Laramie. I'd like a fresh horse please. This one is played out."

"Where's Henry with the mail?" came the curt response.

"Back at Ficklin's Springs, sick."

"Sick?" The way the man scoffed indicated it was an unacceptable excuse.

"Yes, sir. James McArdle thinks its fever and ague."

The announcement was met with silence for a moment.

"Where's the mail?"

"Back a ways, I guess," Sam said, motioning toward the east.

"We'll need better than that," the man demanded.

Had it been daylight, the man would have seen Sam's eyes draw hard. This man didn't give two bits about Henry being sick or Sam's mission. It would take a good deal of luck for him to get any help from this station.

"I can't say where the mail is for certain, except that I found Henry sick with fever on the road between Chimney Rock and Ficklin's Springs. He said the horse dumped him and run off. He was poor enough, I had to let him ride my horse to Ficklin's Springs."

Ignoring Sam, the man shouted back inside the building. "Ben! Get out here, and get on your horse. You've got some back tracking to do."

The last remark carried a suggestion of resentment.

Promptly, a much smaller figure exited the station. In an apparent hurry to finish dressing, the man named Ben quickly moved across the yard toward what Sam figured was the stable and ducked inside.

"I was hoping to get a horse from you all," Sam said again, trying to refocus the conversation on his mission.

"What's wrong with the one you got?"

"Like I said, I already rode him clear from Mud Springs," Sam responded. "He's played out."

For a moment the man rubbed his pointed chin. "I don't know," came his unsettled reply. "These horses are for the mail, and mules are supposed to be for the stages."

Sam couldn't believe what he was hearing. After all the rotten luck he'd had since leaving Mud Springs, now he was up against a simpleminded station keeper who couldn't take his mind off the mail. Sensing that an argument wouldn't help him get a fresh horse, Sam suppressed his exasperation.

"Sir, I got a note here from James McArdle at Mud Springs. We've already lost one rider to the fever. If I don't get to Fort Laramie for some medicine, there'll be more company men die."

Sam pulled the now soggy note from his front pocket and handed it to the station keeper.

"Need a match, Zach?" the third man who had been harnessing the wagon asked.

Zach grunted his assent, and the man pulled a match from his smoking pouch. Once struck, fire leapt from the stick and created a small halo of light in the darkness. The stage man moved the match near, and Zach's squinting eyes darted as he read the note. Sam could see Zach had a crisp mustache and a baldhead. His lips habitually moved as he read the short note. Having satisfied himself, Zach returned it to Sam.

"Well, I suppose that since you work for the company, I could have one of my boys catch up a fresh horse for you."

"I'd appreciate that," Sam said.

"Tom!" Zach shouted back inside the station. "Come and catch up another horse. We got a man out here needing to go to Horse Creek."

Finally confident he would get remounted, Sam slid off Blazer, into the dust of the yard. The horse's head was low, and its body streaked with sweat from the long ride. However, it's eyes were still sharp, and Sam realized the horse could go even farther if put to the task. Although generally not given to tenderness toward animals, Sam took a few moments to pet the loyal horse on the neck.

The blaze-faced sorrel had come nearly fifty miles since leaving Mud Springs ten hours earlier. It had given its best and allowed Sam to carry the message this far. If his message, and ultimately, the life-saving medicine, had any chance of getting through, it would be by the effort of the horses he rode. Curiously, the thought gave Sam confidence. He realized that although people along the line had failed, Blazer never had.

A good horse is funny like that.

CHAPTER 15

Under Zach's watchful eye, the Scott's Bluff station was a scene of order and efficiency. Although not intending to send out two horses in the morning darkness, several loose horses were standing nearby, and it didn't take long for Tom to come jogging back with a black horse at the end of the lariat. The lanky horse had big feet and its long legs made it look like a good traveler. Dutifully, Tom, who looked to be a year or so older than Sam, changed out the saddle and bridle, and in a few minutes he had the new horse ready for Sam. During that time, Zach had invited Sam in for a swallow of coffee, which the tired rider was supremely grateful for. Pressed for time, Sam swallowed down two cups since he didn't know how long it would be before he got another.

In less than twenty minutes from the time he arrived, Sam was back in the saddle and pointed west. The black must have been an experienced horse on the trail because it never hesitated as it started the trip. Some horses loved to run, and the black seemed to be one of those horses. Instead of allowing the horse to push the pace so hard, Sam pulled back gently on the bit to encourage the horse to slow. At first, the horse fought, but Sam kept at it, and eventually they were traveling in an easy swinging lope. It was a pace Sam knew the black could hold all the way to Horse Creek station. If they experienced any problems there, it would still have enough wind to make the next station.

After a full hour on the road, the stars were just beginning to disappear when Sam saw what appeared to be the station at Horse Creek. In the yard, there was the shadowy form of a slim man moving about. There was another dusky figure of a hitched horse that had its ears perked in Sam's direction. It looked like Horse Creek would be an easy switch.

Uncertainty spread over the man's dark face as Sam stopped the black horse in the yard. Apparently, the station keeper knew the horse, but the smooth-faced rider was a stranger.

"Morning," the station keeper greeted Sam skeptically. "What's your business?"

"Morning. I'm carrying a message from Mud Springs, and I'd be obliged to have the horse you've got saddled, sir."

"Lot's of men would like to have these horses, son. Just who are you?"

"Name's Sam Payne. I'm a stock tender at Mud Springs. They all come down with the fever and are needing help from a doctor. James McArdle sent me to Fort Laramie. I've got a note if you'd like to see it."

Sam reached in his pocket to draw out the pulpy note.

Cautious about the stranger reaching into his pockets, the man deferred.

"Where's Ben with the mail?"

"Henry Wright was sick and lost the mail on the road, sir. Ben had to go back and find it."

"Lost the mail?" The man's face registered the news as an impossibility. "Where at?"

"Between Chimney Rock and Ficklin's Springs."

The man's face contorted just a bit as he tried to make sense of the change in situation. In a hurry, Sam pushed the conversation.

"Ben should be along with the mail sometime this morning, but, like I said, I've got some sick friends back at Mud Springs. I'm in an awful hurry for Fort Laramie. I work for the company if that matters at all."

"Well, I guess," the man stammered as he tried to make up his mind. "Let's go ahead and take a look at that note quick."

Sam again reached in his pocket, grabbed the paper, and handed it to the station keeper. The man struck a match that flared and created a small orb of light. For a few seconds, Sam could see his eyes intensely scanning the page for information. Satisfied, he shook out the match and handed the note back.

"Looks, good," he said. "Though, to tell you the truth, I can't read none anyhow."

Fatigued as he was, Sam almost cracked a smile.

"Here you are, son," he said, exchanging reins with Sam. "You say Ben will be around this morning?"

"I'd look for him in a few hours at least. My guess is Henry's horse wouldn't run too far."

"You need something to eat, young 'un? My woman has got breakfast on the stove."

93

He motioned to the soddy, where Sam noticed a woman bustling about inside. Oddly enough, he thought he even saw a child's head peer out from around the corner.

"No, thanks," Sam replied. "I better keep on moving."

Satisfied, the station keeper nodded and bid Sam good luck.

Sam was now mounted on a small buckskin horse. Judging by the way it was built, it was another California-bred horse. Henry had once told him that the further west a body got on the Pony Express, the more California-bred horses were used. Blazer had been a California-bred horse, and Sam could only hope the buckskin would be just as good.

He started his leg from Horse Creek to Cold Springs in the same way he had left Scott's Bluff. Although the buckskin wasn't as determined to run as the black had been, Sam kept it at a pace they could easily keep for the distance between stations. As usual, the land was flat in the valley. The sky was finally blushing shades of pink that signaled sunrise was quickly approaching. As the sky lit, Sam could see rugged buttes drifting to the south. North of the river was a plain covered with grass cured by the summer's sun. With the coming of the new day came the song of the birds as they woke. Somewhere in the distance, he heard a coyote howl. The new dawn brought fresh hope. Hope the exchanges would go well. Hope for good weather. And, hope the doctor at Fort Laramie would be able to help.

He made the trip of fifteen miles in good time, and although lathered up, the buckskin still had plenty of life in him by the end of its run. Along the way, Sam had passed a freight outfit headed east, but other than that, the trail had been unusually lonely. It was still early morning when he saw the next station come into view. Like all the other stations, Cold Springs was a simple affair. Dutifully, the station keeper had a horse ready and waiting for the mail when Sam arrived. After an exchange similar to the one at Horse Creek, Sam was back in the saddle, mounted on a good bay.

His last three exchanges had all gone according to plan, and Sam was making good time. Since leaving Scott's Bluff, he'd ridden around thirty miles, and it had taken him less than three hours. He had managed to get in front of the mail, and he hoped the exchange at Badeau's Ranch would go as smooth. If that was the case, he could hope to be in Fort Laramie for breakfast.

As he rode, Sam felt like he was being rocked to sleep. The combination of birds singing, hooves clopping, exhaustion, and the soft heat of the newly-risen sun were slowly luring him to doze in the saddle. Once or twice, he caught himself nodding off. After snapping back awake and scolding himself, he would try and shake the drowsiness away. It did little to help, and within a few minutes, he would be nodding off again. Obediently, the bay horse followed the road as its rider drifted in and out of sleep. The bay continued to follow the road toward a small rise. Sam again had to shake himself awake.

Wake up, Sam again scolded himself.

Within a few seconds, he felt his eyelids sagging once again. The bay continued up and over the rise and down the backside. As it did, something caught Sam's attention out of the corner of his nearly closed eyes. Groggily, he struggled to open his eyes to see what it was. What he saw caused his eyes to shoot wide open, and he was at full attention.

A long rifle shot away, spread out near a small creek, was a bustling Indian village.

Primary Source Extension:
The following entry comes from Richard Francis Burton's book *City of the Saints.*

> *"A little to the left rose the aerial blue core of that noble landmark, Laramie Peak, based like a mass of solidified air upon a dark wall, the Black Hills, and lit up with the roseate hues of the morning. The distance was about sixty miles; you would have guessed twenty. On the right lay a broad valley, bounded by brown rocks and a plain-colored distance, with the stream winding through it like a thread of quicksilver; in places it was hidden from sight by thickets of red willow, cypress clumps, and dense cool cotton-woods. All was not still life; close below us rose the white lodges of the Ogalala tribe."*

CHAPTER 16

A cold feeling rushed through Sam's body. His thoughts flashed back to Chimney Rock and the horse thieves. Now, with a whole village within sight, a dread inside him told him he was in trouble. Caught out in the open, however, there wasn't anything he could do except continue his course. Maybe they hadn't seen him, and he could get away without drawing attention to himself.

Just as that hope sprang up, it was shot down. A few of the village dogs were hunting mice on the creek and were taken by surprise when the bay loped into view. Defensively, they broke into a series of barks and menacing growls that attracted the attention of more dogs from the village. Within seconds, there were dozens of dogs dashing through the village toward the commotion. This of course, roused the attention of all the Indians as well, who turned their attention toward Sam on the road.

Sam's heart beat fast, and his breath quickened. Months ago, when he'd traveled west with the freighters, he'd been chased by Indians on his trip from Nebraska City, and had only been saved by his wagon boss. Now, he was all alone.

Instead of mounting on their horses to chase him down, Sam saw that most simply returned to what they had been doing. Not one of them appeared to get excited even in the least bit. As the dogs continued their barking, Sam heard a chorus of angry shouts and at least one high-pitched yelp. It wasn't until he and the bay had put more space between themselves and the village that Sam felt his nerves finally calm. Why they didn't chase him down, Sam had no idea.

Never can figure an Indian, I guess, he reasoned to himself.

Onward he and the bay loped across the prairie. Gradually, they lost sight of the Indian village, but a new set of structures rose up in front of them. Sam suspected it was Badeau's Station. As he loped closer, he noticed it was busier than the others. Pulling the sweating bay back to a trot, Sam trotted closer to the yard.

Around the collection of buildings were at least two-dozen people doing some morning business. Some were whites, some were Indians, and some looked somewhere in between. A few ragged and bone-thin horses were ground hitched by the largest structure. Others were staked and hobbled in the grass to the south. A freighter's train was just pulling out as he was riding in, and the dust it kicked up provided a fresh layer on the people and buildings, which all looked to have already accumulated many layers in the past.

In front of the station, several men lounged and smoked their pipes in the morning's comfortable heat. Although they appeared to be white, Sam noticed they were wearing the fringed buckskin that was popular with the Indians. Each had a long rifle lying nearby that was dirtied from years of use and abuse. Their hair dangled past their shoulders, and it matched their generally scruffy appearance.

Sam trotted the bay up to the building and dismounted near the group. The men stopped their conversation to turn a suspicious eye on the tired-looking rider. Having learned that a timid disposition would get him nothing but trouble, Sam spoke directly to the group.

"Station keeper around?"

For a moment, Sam was met with nothing but the sucking sound as the men smoked their pipes. Then, casually, a man in a beaten wide-brimmed black hat that slouched nearly to his shoulders motioned with his head.

"Bordeaux's inside," he said in a voice that sounded like the iron rim of a wagon wheel crushing gravel. "You come huntin' directions, tenderfoot? Nebraska City is thataway," the man gestured east.

"I come from Nebraska City last spring," Sam replied. "I'm headed to Fort Laramie, and I don't think I'll need directions."

"We'll see," the man remarked as he exhaled blue smoke.

Dropping the reins of the bay, Sam stepped past the group and headed inside. Although small, the station was more organized than the others he had seen. He could quickly tell this station also served as a trading post. On the walls were shelves of cooking implements, shooting supplies, furs, and eye-catching Indian goods. There were ornamented bags, smoking pipes, painted hides, and beaded moccasins. Inside,

Sam saw several customers, a well-built man, several children, and a well-dressed Indian woman sorting through a pile of furs. It looked to Sam like a well-run business.

"Whatdya' need?" The straightforward question came from the man. His dark complexion was offset by a noticeably white shirt. In a world where everything was brown, black, and dirty, a clean and boiled white shirt was striking. Aside from the shirt, the man had sharp features, a well-trimmed black mustache, and deep-set eyes that seemed to stare right through Sam.

"I ride for the Pony Express, sir, and I'd liked a fresh horse."

Again, Sam retold his story, and that the mail would likely be arriving in a few hours. After the explanation, Sam handed the man the note, which seemed to satisfy his doubts.

"Louie," he ordered one of his half-breed children who looked around twelve years old. "Go fetch the horse in the stable. When you're done, you can catch another for Ben when he comes through."

The small dark-skinned boy nodded and stepped past Sam out of the building. Sam thanked the station keeper and followed him. Outside, the three men still loafed idly on the ground. For a few minutes, Sam had a chance to rest. His body ached and sleep still clung persistently to him, but it was now less than ten miles to Fort Laramie.

And then you can turn around and do it all over again, Sam reminded himself.

Vocabulary:
Tenderfoot – An inexperienced man on the plains.

Primary Source Extension:
The following comes from Richard Francis Burton's book *City of the Saints* about the station.

"At 10 20 A.M. we halted to change mules at Badeau's Ranch, or, as it is more grandiloquently called, "Laramie City." The "city," like many a Western "town," still appertains to the category of things about to be; it is at present represented by a single large "store," with out-houses full of small half-breeds. The principal articles of traffic are liquors and groceries for the whites, and ornaments for the Indians, which are bartered for stock (i.e., animals) and peltries. The prices asked for the skins were from $1– $130 for a fox or a coyote, $ 3 for wolf, bear, or deer, $6— $7 for an elk, $5 for a common buffalo, and from $8 to $35 for the same painted, pictographed, and embroidered. Some of the party purchased moccasins, for which they paid $1-$2; the best articles are made by the Snakes, and when embroidered by white women rise as high as $25. I bought, for an old friend who is insane upon the subject of pipes, one of the fine marble-like sand stone bowls brought from the celebrated Côteau (slope) des Prairies, at the head of Sioux River."

Primary Source Follow Up:
1. What does Richard Burton say some of the party purchased?
2. Does it surprise you that people from the east would have purchased goods from this trading post? Why or why not?
3. If you had been in the stagecoach, what do you think you would have bought? Why?

CHAPTER 17

Louie brought out a sleek strawberry roan with a jug head and knobby knees. At first, Sam had his doubts about the horse. However, Louie didn't say a word and simply grabbed the reins to the saddled horse. After sliding the bit into the horse's mouth, Sam stepped onto the horse

Nearly the instant Sam hit the seat, the roan's muscles tensed. In a split second, the horse ducked its head and took three or four big jumps down the road. Fatigued and surprised, the bucking dislodged Sam from his seat, and he felt himself bouncing further to one side. In desperation, his free hand frantically searched for something to grab to keep his seat. Through the violence of the bucking, his fingers luckily touched the saddle horn. At the instant Sam thought he was saved, the horse made an explosive jump to one side. It was too much for Sam, and in that moment, he abandoned hope of staying in the saddle. With no other choice, he let himself go and fell to the ground.

Dry dust erupted around him as he hit the ground hard. The collision sent a blunt pain through his entire body and forced the air out of his lungs. As the pain flashed, he was aware of the roan continuing its bucking away from him. For just a second, Sam allowed himself to lie in the dust and deal with the throbbing pain. Before it had subsided, he wearily pushed himself to one knee. His breath was short and ragged as he once again tried to fill his lungs with air. After a few seconds, the pain was fading away, and Sam was aware that Louie had already caught the roan and was bringing it back. He could also hear the dry laughter of the three men smoking in front of the store.

Sound of the laughter pricked Sam's pride, and he pushed himself to his feet. He slapped the dust from his clothes, which came out in small little clouds that hung in a foggy vapor around him. Tasting sand in his mouth, he spat the grit out and wiped his face. Casting a glance back toward the three men, he saw their faces were aglow with pleasure.

Glad they enjoyed that, Sam thought sarcastically.

By then, Louie had brought the roan back and was patiently holding the reins for Sam.

"Why didn't you tell me he was a bucker?" Sam asked.

Louie just shrugged his shoulders with indifference. "Most of the Pony riders stay on."

That remark evoked a loud laugh from at least one of the loafers.

"Just give me the horse," Sam said. The boy's remark combined with the laughter of the men caused Sam to forget his pain.

Louie extended the rein to Sam, and Sam once again mounted the roan. This time, he hadn't even made it to the saddle when the horse started to make its dash away. Pulling on the near rein, Sam got the horse to circle into him, which gave him a chance to throw his right leg over. By the time he was in the saddle, the roan resumed its high-spirited bucking.

"Woohoo!" Sam heard one of the loafers shout through the confusion. "Give him a kiss, kid, maybe he'll settle down!"

Like before, the horse coiled, jumped to one side, and then darted back to the other. Its powerful muscles sporadically convulsed as it fought to dislodge the rider from its back. At the same instant its feet left the ground, the roan jerked its head to pull the reins out of Sam's hand. Having won the previous battle, the roan's aggressiveness showed it felt confident it could win once again.

This time though, Sam was ready. He had found his seat and had steadied himself with the saddle horn. Realizing he was caught in a test of wills, Sam screwed himself down tight to the saddle and was determined to make the ride. Trying to assert itself, the roan bucked and darted, zigged and zagged, anything to once again beat the adversary on its back. Try as it might, Sam had a good seat and was staying with the bucking horse.

Instead of abusing the roan with bit and spurs like he had done the day before to the sorrel, Sam just tried to endure the storm. When the horse darted one way, Sam prodded it back to the other with spur and rein. When the horse made another sideways dash, Sam did the same until the roan began to submit. Although Sam didn't want to thrash the horse, he had no intention of letting it win. Instead, Sam fought the roan tooth and nail until it complied. When it did, Sam gave it freedom to travel easily. After several steps the defiant horse would revert back to its antics, at which time Sam again poked, prodded, and pulled, until he got the response he wanted. It didn't take long before the exertion had the roan gasping for air. As the roan tired, its rebellion weakened as well.

In a long minute, Sam had the roan under his control. Victoriously, he trotted the bucker compliantly past by the three loafing men.

"Not bad for a tenderfoot," the man in the black hat remarked.

"Might even make Fort Laramie," Sam replied with a broad smile on his face.

"Might," the man replied, unwillingly to admit defeat.

"Only one way to find out. See you fellers on the turnaround," Sam said as he confidently tipped his hat.

With that, he prodded the roan and was soon dashing away toward Fort Laramie.

Vocabulary
Jug Head – Referring to a horse that has a long-rectangular head.

CHAPTER 18

After the initial rebellion, the red roan settled down and loped over the dusty road. The sun was just beginning to warm, and it took the cool freshness of the morning with it when it did. Overhead, the blue sky was dotted with puffs of white clouds across its vast dominion. Far off in the distance, one of those white clouds hovered above a tall-tapered peak rising above the rest. Sam had heard stories of the Black Hills west of Fort Laramie. He suspected that was the name of the ragged range outlined on the skyline. Even from a distance, the peaks triggered a feeling of adventure and allure. For a few miles, Sam afforded his mind a break from his responsibility, and he let his imagination take him to those rugged mountains. In his mind, it was a wild and primeval place. Letting his mind run free refreshed him in a way he couldn't have explained. In fact, he had gotten so wrapped up in his dreams that by the time the buildings of Fort Laramie were close enough to see, he couldn't remember the seven miles he had already crossed. With the fort in view, Sam refocused on his mission.

A few hundred yards from the fort, the road descended down a gentle slope and crossed a wide and clear-flowing stream. Riding up out of the shallow bottom, Sam gained a clear view of what lay ahead. Surrounding the fort was nothing but naked prairie, broken hills covered with sagebrush, and Indian tipis. At the center of it all was a collection of buildings.

Most of the buildings were small, single-story, and rectangular in shape. From a distance, these buildings seemed an assortment of adobe, rock, sod, and wooden structures. A few rose two stories in height, giving the fort an air of civilization. There also appeared to be a large rectangular open space in the center of the grounds. A large American flag fluttering atop a flagpole dominated this open area. Like ants scuttling in the dirt, Sam saw blue-coated soldiers moving about the entire grounds, engaged in one task or another. One particular group was marching around the open area in cadence to the booming voice of their commander.

In addition to the military personnel, Sam saw several freighting wagons parked near what he could only guess was a mercantile. Teams of tired mules stood hip-shot while freighters busily loaded and unloaded freight into and out of the wagons they pulled. A handful of Indians mingled among the collection of other people at the fort as well. Some of these were bare-chested men with long-black braids stretching down to the small of the their backs. In stark contrast to the uniformed soldiers, these copper-skinned men strolled the grounds with only a small piece of material covering their groin. A few Indian women also roved across the grounds. In their long buckskin dresses, these women were easy to pick apart from the men. If the dresses didn't give them away as women, the naked children curiously shadowing them might.

Nearing what appeared to be a stable at the entrance of the fort, Sam saw a uniformed man absorbed in some morning business. Dressed in a dirty white shirt and blue pants, the man's curly brown hair protruding from beneath his cocked <u>forage cap</u> matched the hair of his drooping mustache.

"Morning," Sam greeted as he rode up. "Do you know where I can find the doctor?"

The soldier turned to look at him. The glaze in his blue eyes revealed what Sam interpreted as disinterest. "You sick?" he drawled.

"No, sir. My friends at Mud Springs are."

For a second, the man just chewed on a cheek full of tobacco. Judging by the brown spots on his white shirt, Sam suspected the soldier chewed tobacco regularly. After a few seconds, the soldier spat a dark stream of spit and then motioned with his head.

"He'll be behind the <u>sutler</u>'s store back thataways."

With that, the solider turned back to whatever idle work Sam had interrupted.

Without so much as a thank you, Sam nudged the roan up the road in the direction the man had motioned. Along the way, he directed the horse past a series of buildings. The smell of baking bread mixed with the more general smells of horse and sweat as he rode up and around the sutler's store. As he rounded the corner, another stone building came into view. This one didn't appear as busy, and Sam suspected it was the hospital. He had finally made it. Now, Sam just hoped they would be able to help him.

After riding over, Sam dismounted and tied the roan to a hitching rail at the front of the modest building. After being in a saddle for nearly 21 hours straight, his legs and back were stiff, but he hobbled as quickly as he could through the front door. Inside, the building was not dark, but not bright either. It had a few cots, some medical equipment on the wall, and a few other instruments that informed Sam he had indeed found the correct building. Behind a small desk, sat a man in a simple wooden chair. He was a young looking man who lacked the hard lines on his face that people developed early on the frontier. His neatly trimmed hair and beard showed no gray, but something about his appearance gave a feeling of distinction. As Sam entered the room, the man looked up from some papers that littered the desk.

"Good morning," he said in greeting.

"Mornin'," Sam replied. "I've come to see if I could talk to a doctor."

"That's me. I'm Doctor Johns," came the reply.

The statement caused Sam to hesitate for a moment. He'd been expecting to see a gray-bearded man in wire-rimmed glasses, not a young and active person.

"You?" Sam asked.

"What can I do for you?" Dr. Johns responded, bypassing the question.

"Well, I've got some sick friends back at Mud Springs. James McArdle is the Pony Express station keeper there, and he sent me."

"How sick?"

"Bad. One man has already died, three more are laid up in bed, and another may soon be."

109

Anxiously, the doctor stood up from his chair. He had an honest urgency in his eyes when he spoke.

"What are their symptoms?"

"They've got a fever, chills, and can't hardly stay awake. Mr. McArdle told me it was fever and ague."

"Hmm," Dr. John's hand moved to his chin as he thought. "A bit late for fever and ague. Are you sure it isn't the cholera?"

Sam didn't know much about diseases. "How could you tell?" he asked.

"Well, if they are vomiting and have terrible diarrhea, it may be cholera."

Sam thought back for a moment. "No, none of that. They just got the fever and lay up in bed all day."

For a moment, Dr. Johns seemed to roll the possibilities over in his mind. Sam felt helpless just standing there. He wished he'd known more about sickness, but all he knew was that they had fever, chills, and tiredness. Not knowing what else to say seemed to make the whole thing worse.

After a few moments, the doctor sighed heavily. "Although the night air is not generally as harmful this time of year, I suppose we'll have to go on what Mr. McArdle says."

"Do you have some medicine?" Sam asked.

"Oh yes," the doctor nodded vigorously. "Although our air is not as bad as it is further east, we still get our share of fever and ague from time to time. How many do you believe have it?"

"Well, there is Luke, Mr. McArdle, Henry, and maybe Dan," Sam replied. "Four. That's all for right now."

"Ok. Give me a few minutes to get the quinine made up. If you'd like, you might head over to the sutler's store. They generally have coffee on the boil this time of day and maybe some breakfast. You look like you have had a long ride."

110

Sam nodded in affirmation. He *had* had a long ride, and he *was* tired, but he did not want to loiter about. As soon as the medicine was ready, he was determined to leave.

"How long do you suppose you'll be?" Sam asked.

"A quarter of an hour at least."

"Ok," Sam replied. "I'll be back in a quarter of an hour then. Thank you."

Waving his hand to acknowledge the gratitude, the doctor turned to prepare the medicine.

Sam turned and walked out of the cool rock building into the morning sun. The August sun was growing hot, and a few flies and gnats buzzed around like the constant irritation they were. It would be a long ride back to Mud Springs. If things went well, though, Sam expected he could be back by nightfall.

IF things go well, Sam reminded himself.

Vocabulary:

Forage Cap – A soft cap, usually having a stiff brim, which made up part of a soldier's uniform.

Sutler – A person who sells provisions to army soldiers.

CHAPTER 19

On tired legs, Sam walked toward the sutler's store. He followed the path across the open space, crossed the main road, before rounding the corner of the store. Lit by the morning sun, the limestone wall was bright, but not nearly as bright as the white painted window and door frames embedded in it. Fanning out in front of the store was a large half circle of bare dirt where the grass had been trampled. Like the hub of a wagon wheel, the dirt patch was the meeting place of a number of smaller paths that broke off in various directions. A group of men dressed in eastern clothes emerged from the far door, before heading to a stagecoach parked not far away. Unsure of which door to use, Sam decided to try the door the group had exited. After crossing the dirt patch, Sam turned the porcelain door handle and stepped into the room.

Inside, the store was open and bright from the light that poured in through the glass windows. Like many similar buildings, the sutler's store was full of trade goods of all kinds. Unlike some of the other trading posts, this one was neatly organized. Stacks of cloth, cooking utensils, knives, and shooting supplies were all showcased behind a large cottonwood counter. The counter was three feet wide, the color of butter, and had been polished smooth from many transactions. Behind that counter, stood a man dressed in a white apron. He had a broad face with a neatly trimmed chocolate brown mustache. The look he gave Sam was not cold, but not overly friendly either.

"Morning," Sam greeted the man.

"Morning," came the reply. "What can I do for you?"

"I come from Mud Springs to see the doctor about some medicine. He told me you might have some coffee and a bite to eat."

"Oh, did he?" Sam picked up a faint irritation in the man's voice. "You a paying customer?"

"I ain't got any money, if that's what you're asking."

Like people do when breaking bad news, the man let out a sigh. "Well, I can set you up with a cup of coffee, but I can't be handing out free meals to every dusty rider that comes limping in here. You can understand that I'm sure."

Sam nodded. "Yes, sir. I'd appreciate the coffee all the same."

"Aw, Mark," interrupted a stern voice. "Give the man some antelope steak at least."

Sam turned and saw a solitary man in buckskin pants and a red flannel shirt sitting at a small table in the corner. He had a battered-brown hat that nearly matched his deeply tanned skin. Propped in the corner nearby was a large caliber rifle that Sam could tell had seen plenty of use.

"How I run my business, isn't any business of yours, Jem," the man behind the counter replied.

The man called Jem turned his attention from his meal toward Mark. When he did, Sam saw a face that looked like it had been chiseled from granite. Deep lines creasing it revealed that Jem was middle-aged. Across his cheek was a noticeable scar. It was a few inches long and was paler than the sunburned skin surrounding it. His eyes were neither menacing nor friendly. They were like the eyes of a watchdog guarding a home. They were alert, clear, and knowing.

"I believe that antelope steak is my business, Mark."

"Not once I pay you for the carcass it ain't."

"Maybe not, but the next one will be before I sell it to ya'."

"What are you saying, Jem?"

Jem wiped a bit of food that clung to his lip. "I'm saying give the young man an antelope steak, Mark. By God, look at him. Looks like he had a hard ride if ever a man has."

"Loafers are like flies, Jem. You never seen just one at a free meal."

"Ain't gonna be free, Mark. You're gonna pay for it."

"Me? I won't pay for it."

"Ah, I think you will. See if you don't feed him, I might just keep that in mind when I bring meat in next time. Game is gettin' mighty scarce 'round here, Mark. Us hunters been needin' to go further and further to keep you satisfied. Price of meat might be risin', if you catch my meanin'."

Caught between the two men, Sam didn't like knowing he was the cause of the tension.

"It's really alright, mister," Sam said to Jem. "I work at Mud Springs and understand what goes in to making a living out here."

For the first time, Jem turned his attention to Sam. As the hard eyes fixed on him, Sam wished he had just kept quiet.

"True enough," Jem said after a second. "But there's more to livin' than dollars and cents."

For a few long seconds, silence hung in the air like a heavy fog. The rawhide backed chair creaked slightly when Jem turned his attention back to Mark.

"Go get him a steak, Mark. The man's hungry."

Cussing under his breath, Mark turned and crossed the dirt floor toward a door to a back room. After he left, Sam turned to Jem and spoke.

"Thank you, mister, but you didn't have to do that."

"You're right about that," Jem said as he turned his attention back to the last few bites on his own plate. "Sit down if you have a mind."

Tired as he was, Sam did have a mind to sit. He grabbed another chair that had a rawhide back and seat, moved it toward the table, and sat down. For the first few seconds, the relief of sitting was one of the greatest feelings Sam could ever remember. Although Sam had experienced plenty of work and hardship, he couldn't recall a time when he appreciated sitting in a chair as much as he did at that moment. Jem seemed to recognize the situation and quietly continued to feed himself.

For almost a minute, they sat without a word passing. Then from behind him, Sam heard the shuffling of feet. He turned to see Mark bringing a plate in one hand and a steaming cup in the other. The tinware made a clatter as the sutler set it on the table. Without a word, Mark turned his back and retreated behind the cottonwood counter. On the

115

plate was part of an antelope steak that had been cooked earlier that morning and a loaf of bread that had a few bites missing. Despite its unpleasant appearance, Sam picked up the fork and knife and started in like a starved wolf.

As he ate, he was thinking about the stranger across the table from him. While working for the freighting outfit, Sam had befriended an older man named Baker. As a seasoned frontiersman, Baker had often taken to yarnin' at night around the fire. He had come west after the first wagon trains in the 40s and had traveled much of the unexplored West. Oftentimes, he'd spoken of a companion by the name Jemmey Fletcher. According to Baker, Jemmey had been a trapper in the early days before the first wagon trains had ever gone to Oregon. Fletcher had fought Indians, trapped beaver, hunted buffalo, and maybe knew as much about the West as any man. Although the small man at the table didn't fit the image Sam had created in his mind, his confident manner led Sam to suspect it might be the same person. Curiosity was too much for Sam to hold back.

"Thanks for the steak," he said between a mouthful of meat and bread.

"You looked like you could stand it," Jem replied, keeping his attention to his own plate.

"If you don't mind me asking, your name is Jem?"

"Yep. Has been all my life."

"You wouldn't be Jemmey Fletcher would you?"

There was a brief pause before Jem looked up at him.

"I would be," Jemmey said curtly.

Tired as he was, Sam felt a mix of both excitement and relief. Having heard so much about Jemmey, Sam no longer felt like he was sitting next to a stranger.

"You ever met a man named Baker?"

"Ha! Met him?" Jemmey's face instantly lit up. "I ate more <u>buffler</u> with that <u>coon</u> than you could eat in a year. How do you know Andrew?"

"Andrew? I only ever knew him as Baker."

"Oh, his name is Andrew all right. Mother named him after Andrew Jackson who won the Battle of New Orleans. How you know him?"

"I worked on a freighting outfit with him this past spring."

"Oh. He's still beatin' on them oxen is he?"

Sam chuckled a little at the exaggeration. "Yeah, he is."

"I'll have to admit, I never did imagine Andrew would walk that trail as many times as he has. Sounds like it's keeping him alive at least. How'd you come to know me?"

"Baker talked about you a good deal."

"Well, now," Jem scoffed, "Don't believe half the lies that ol' coon told you. He could lie with the best of them."

Jemmey's vigor was contagious, and Sam laughed again.

"He spoke very highly of you."

"Well, I'll speak very highly of him as well. If it warn't for him, I'd <u>have lost my hair</u> on a few occasions. You done well if you listened to what Andrew told you."

Sam put another bite of antelope steak in his mouth. It was cold and tough, but it was food.

"I never did catch your name," Jem said.

"Sam Payne," Sam replied through the meat.

"Any special reason you look so wore out, Sam?"

Sam swallowed the meat and drank some coffee. The question brought him back to his responsibility unexpectedly quick.

117

"I work for the Pony Express out of Mud Springs. Yesterday, I rode into the station and they were all sick. I had to come here to see about getting some medicine."

The bad news caused Jem to shake his head unhappily as if he knew the people.

"You left Mud Springs yesterday? Must be bad for you to ride that fast."

Sam nodded. Something hard formed in his throat just before he replied.

"Willy died."

Again, Jemmey gloomily shook his head. "Sorry to hear that. Maybe one day them folks back east will figure out how to stop them sicknesses. You riding back soon?"

Sam nodded as he stuffed another bite of food into his mouth. "Uh huh. Just as soon as the doctor gets the medicine ready."

"Well, good luck to you, Sam. It'll take some <u>sand</u> to make a ride like that."

Sam didn't know what to say, so he just nodded. Having felt a brief release from his responsibility, talk of his friends brought back the continuous worry and anxiety he'd felt since leaving Mud Springs. Impatient to be back on the move, Sam stuffed another bite of meat into his mouth and washed it down with the last of the coffee. He grabbed what was left of the bread, and decided to eat it on his walk back to the hospital.

"Been nice meeting you, Mr. Fletcher," Sam said as he stood up from his chair.

"Just Jem, Sam," Jemmey replied as he extended his hand. "Pleased to meet you, too, and I hope you get that medicine back in time.

They shook hands. Then, without another word, Sam walked on stiff legs toward the door.

With over 100 more miles of riding ahead of him, he knew he'd have to make the ride of his life if the medicine were to get there in time.

Vocabulary:
Yarnin – Telling stories.
Buffler – Buffalo.
Coon – A friendly term used by mountain men.
Lost my hair – Been scalped.
Sand – Toughness.

CHAPTER 20

After leaving the sutler's store, Sam headed back to the hospital across the same faint trail. As he made his way, his thoughts turned back to Luke and Henry. He knew Henry was sick, but if he got medicine this morning, he would likely be ok. He couldn't be so sure about Luke. For all Sam knew, the Mud Springs crew was digging another grave this morning. Mentioning Willy to Jemmey had reopened some feelings in Sam that the exertion of his ride had dulled. Like bright-red blood flows from a picked scab, the sting of Willy's death resurfaced. As the wound reopened, Sam did his best to cover it back up. It would do no good to wallow in his sadness. Instead, he had to keep moving forward. Although a life had been lost, there was still a life to be saved. With renewed resolve, Sam opened the door to the hospital.

Dr. Johns was just finishing up as he walked in.

"Ah, you're back," he greeted Sam as he walked over. "I have everything ready for you. If they really have the fever and ague, then this quinine should do the trick."

Sam nodded, as he accepted the small envelope the medicine had been placed in. The doctor had also managed to wrap it with a small bit of oiled silk. "What should I do with it?" Sam asked.

"Give a small dose of the powder to anybody showing signs of the sickness. They should improve in a day or two. They can take another helping in a day or two if signs persist."

"Thank you," Sam replied. "I'm sorry I can't pay you."

The young doctor shook his head. "No need to apologize. This fort operates to protect and aid the sons and daughters of the United States. It's also my duty as a doctor to tend those in the Shepherd's flock in need of help. I just hope the medicine gets there in time."

"Thank you, Dr. Johns," Sam said as he extended his hand.

"My pleasure," Dr. Johns replied as he shook Sam's hand. "You best be going. You've got a long ride ahead of you."

Leaving the hospital, Sam walked over to the red roan standing lazily at the hitching rail. He'd only ridden the roan half of a leg on the way in, and he knew the horse had plenty of lungs for another eight miles back to Badeau's. Unhitching the horse, then stepping up in the stirrup, Sam reined the horse back down the trail he had ridden in on. Setting the horse into a comfortable lope, Sam coasted past the buildings and people of Fort Laramie. In the matter of a few seconds, he raced past the grumpy soldier at the stable and was back on the prairie.

After fording the river, Sam rode up the bank and back onto the level prairie. As he did, the familiar landscape opened up in front of him. On the north side, a few broken hills speckled with white rock gleamed in the sun. On the southern horizon, a low cedar-covered ridge formed the skyline. In between, the open prairie seemed to taunt him in challenge. The grass danced wildly in the southern wind that was starting to blow. The tract of land ahead of him was big; too big for a man on foot. On his own, there was no way he would cross the one hundred miles back to Mud Springs in time. However, with the Pony Express it could be done. The natural fleetness of the horse and the ambition of man had come together on this road to overcome the nagging enemy of distance. Steam was overcoming that barrier further east, but on the frontier, it was still left to the ancient alliance of man and horse. Atop the roan, with the sweeping view of the endless prairie challenging him, Sam finally appreciated the worth of the animal he rode. Alone, Sam would fail. Together, they could go anywhere.

In spite of the speed the Pony Express offered, Sam knew making it back to Mud Springs would not be easy. By the end of the day, he'd need to ride to the horizon, beyond the horizon, *beyond* the horizon. Badeau's, Cold Springs, Horse Creek, Scott's Bluff, Ficklin's Springs, Chimney Rock, and then Court House Station. Sam could only hope the station keepers had enough sense to understand that today he'd be coming back through and that they would have a horse ready for him. Realizing that might not be the case, Sam reminded himself of what he had learned so far. He vowed not to make the same mistakes again.

In less than an hour, he had ridden eight miles and saw Badeau's come into view. Trail traffic had been light, and he'd only passed the stagecoach and a team of freighters he had seen early that morning. To his relief, in the yard of the station he saw Louie walking out of the stable with a horse saddled and ready. The roan was sweating but still willing to run as Sam entered the yard. Pulling back on the reins, the roan skidded to a halt in a cloud of dust. Stepping off to one side, Sam quickly switched horses with Louie who was holding another red roan with a wild eye.

Not wanting another surprise, Sam asked, with a bit of a grin, "This one buck?"

Louie shook his head while maintaining a blank face. "No. He's a runner, though."

Nodding, Sam crossed to the horse's left side and stepped in the stirrup. The three men loafing outside the station hadn't moved at all since Sam had left, and he could see he'd drawn their attention. Feeling a little prideful, he touched the brim of his hat and shouted, "Made it back alright!"

In response, the man in the black hat shouted back, "Looks like you're headed in the right direction: east!"

"Least I'm headed somewhere!" Sam shouted back. Then he turned and spurred the fresh roan down the road.

The loafer's response was too muffled by the sound of wind and pounding hooves for Sam to hear it. It didn't really matter anyway. All that mattered was the next eleven miles to Cold Springs. Sam hoped his luck carried with him as he went.

Although Louie had tricked him with the first horse, he'd been plain honest about the second. The wild-eyed roan could run. The problem was the horse seemed scared of everything. As a result, keeping him centered down the road was a major challenge. Sam couldn't tell if it was spooked by the wind, the shadows, or if it was just the animal's nature. Instead of traveling straight, the horse seemed determined to weave from one side to the other searching for a better route.

It was also one of the quickest horses Sam had ever ridden. As the horse darted from side to side, it took all Sam's attention to stay centered in the saddle.

Feels like riding a snake, Sam thought to himself as the horse made another dash across the road.

After the first mile, the roan began to settle down, but it still took a meandering course down the road. They hadn't traveled another mile, when Sam saw the Indian village scattered along the creek. Off to one side, a few Indian riders were loping their horses in the grass between Sam and the tipis. Even from a distance, Sam could tell they had spotted him. One of the riders pointed the <u>flea-bitten gray</u> horse they were riding in Sam's direction. It looked as if the rider was aiming for a spot where they would meet Sam on the road. Three more riders turned their horses and followed the leader. As they rode to intercept him, the Indians' long-black braids streamed behind them.

Sam's heart beat a little faster. If they meant him harm, there was little he could do on the open road. Cautiously, he let one hand hover near the revolver in his belt. Alone on the trail, the last thing he wanted was a fight, but he couldn't turn back. There was too much depending on this ride. He kept the roan pointed east, to meet whatever they had in store for him.

Over the next minute, the drama played itself out across the open prairie. Sam continued to ride the roan east; the four riders galloped north toward the road. Everything had been in their favor, and soon, they had beaten him to a spot in the road. Once they had arrived, they stopped their horses in a straight line at the edge of the road. The riders' features became clearer as Sam loped closer.

They appeared to be boys, bare-chested and clothed only in a small buckskin loincloth, with simple moccasins on their dangling feet. Aside from those simple articles, their copper skin was exposed to wind, rain, and sun. Their bodies were lean and well muscled, and their long-black braids danced in the stiff-southern wind. Each sat bareback atop a small and shaggy pony. As Sam rode closer, he could see that a simple strand of rawhide wrapped around the pony's jaw was the only horse tack they used. Although plain clothed with primitive horse gear, the riders looked like princes of the prairie.

However lordly they looked, Sam's heart beat faster as he approached the waiting horsemen. The roan, too, seemed extra edgy and began to prance more and more. If Sam was going to meet a group of attacking Indians, he wished he could have done it on a horse that was a little easier to ride. Only a few seconds now separated them, and the Indians looked as immovable as stone statues waiting for him.

Sam could no longer restrain his hand from settling on the butt of his revolver.

He was riding close now, and the roan swerved to the opposite side. If anything was going to happen, it was going to happen now. Sam's attention was focused completely on the waiting riders. He watched their every move. If this was a trap, he was intent on doing whatever it would take to break through. With less than twenty yards to go, Sam saw one of the boys make the first move.

Slowly, the boy on the flea-bitten gray raised his hand in the air with his fingers spread wide. He followed that gesture by revealing a set of white teeth in a smile. Sam was close enough he could see the boy's obsidian eyes. He had expected to see a vicious look, but instead, the boy's expression couldn't have been friendlier. After the first boy raised his hand and smiled, the others followed suit.

They rode over to say hello? The realization caught Sam off guard.

125

Awkwardly, he lifted his hand from the butt of his revolver, and half returned their greeting. None of the boys moved. Instead, they held their horses in a line, with their hands raised and broad smiles on their faces.

In a cloud of dust, Sam dashed past them. The unexpected greeting had knocked him off balance. Unable to resist the temptation, Sam turned in the saddle to take another look. The line of horsemen was unmoving, and Sam knew he had no reason to fear. Feeling impolite, he raised his hand a little higher in greeting. Turning his attention back to the road and the jittery roan, Sam tried to make sense of what had just happened. After a few minutes, he still hadn't come up with an answer.

With a few miles behind them, the horse finally began to ride straight down the road. In less than an hour, the Cold Springs soddy came into view. Sam could see the station man waiting dutifully with a horse in the yard ready for a switch. As expected, the roan shied to one side as they rode in the yard. Sam got it stopped and managed to get off without any problems.

"Thank you," Sam shouted above the gusting wind.

The man nodded in reply, then shouted back, "You're making good time, young 'un. You got yer medicine?"

"Sure do," Sam replied as he patted the pocket containing the envelope. "I just hope I can get it there in time."

"I hope you do too. Good luck to you!"

Grabbing the reins to a sorrel the man had been holding, Sam stepped aboard and once again headed east. Next stop would be Horse Creek and then Zach's Scott's Bluff Station. Although things had been going off without a hitch so far, the weather was beginning to turn. The wind howled and coursed across the prairie with powerful bursts like waves pounding the shores. A fog of dust rose from the road as the wind stirred the loose soil. Overhead, clouds scuttled across the sky.

I hope it ain't blowing in a storm, Sam wished. Whether it did or not, there was nothing Sam could do to stop it.

Vocabulary:
Flea-bitten gray - A horse or mule with a white undercoat spotted with small dark gray dots all over its body.

Extension Article:
Use the QR code below, or search "Little Aubry" at frontierlife.net to learn about the ride that is generally regarded as the most impressive in Western History.

CHAPTER 21

It was past noon when Sam found himself on the open prairie a few miles from Scott's Bluff station. He'd made an easy switch at Horse Creek. The well-muscled bay he had been given had carried its pace exceptionally well, despite fighting the incessant wind. After over twenty-four hours in the saddle, Sam was tired and thankful for a good horse.

Through the fog of dust being stirred up by the wind, Sam thought he could see a rider coming his way. By the way the rider was moving, Sam knew it was Ben with the mail heading west. Nobody would push a horse that hard unless they knew they had a fresh one waiting not far away. As they rode closer, Sam raised a hand toward him. In turn, Ben raised his hand in response. Neither hesitated for even a single stride. In a moment, they blew past each other like two locomotives chugging down opposite tracks. There was a flurry of commotion as they dashed past each other. Then, in the blink of an eye, all the commotion ended, and each rider was alone again.

Several miles later, Sam was riding into the station at Scott's Bluff. Zach was standing in the yard, with one hand on his head to keep his black hat from flying off. His eyes still carried a suggestion of blame for Sam's inconvenience. Despite the man's irritability, he had prepared for Sam's return. Within a few seconds of arriving, Sam saw Tom exiting the stable with the fresh horse.

There was little ceremony in the exchange. Sam already knew Zach was a stern man who didn't appreciate disruption to his routine. Sam had met more than a few men like that already. Change irritated them, and nothing except return to order would soothe their ruffled feathers. Sam figured Zach wasn't an easy man to work for, but he had still done the honorable thing in having a fresh horse ready.

After a quick, "thanks," Sam grabbed the sorrel horse from Tom and got in the saddle. Turning the horse southeast, he headed toward Scott's Bluff. Approaching in the daylight, Sam could now fully appreciate the towering bluff he had ridden past last night. The white rock that formed its core was bright in the early afternoon sun. Aside from the few mountains Sam had seen, Scott's Bluff was the largest thing he'd ever been around. It rose hundreds of feet into the air, and its immensity dwarfed all that surrounded it. Although dulled from fatigue, for a few minutes the impressive escarpment held Sam's attention. For all the monotony of the plains, there were times it lived up to the legend.

After crossing over the pass, the sorrel traveled smoothly down the decline on the other side. Continuing on, they soon exited the protective rock formation and were blasted by the strong wind once again. Further east, the sky was taking on a hue of deep purple. Low-hanging, granite-gray clouds rushed across the sky like leaves blow over the surface of a pond. Sam thought he saw Brett's freighting outfit camped south of the trail a few hundred yards, but other than that, the plain was empty.

In the distance, the rugged buttes south of Ficklin's Springs rose toward the gray sky. Sight of the buttes gave Sam a sense of accomplishment. Once he reached them, he could get Henry the medicine he needed. Although eager to travel fast, Sam held the sorrel back a little. He didn't want to risk running the horse out too fast. Despite traveling slower than he would have liked, with each step the buttes grew larger and larger until eventually Sam saw the simple sod buildings of Ficklin's Springs.

I hope I'm in time, Sam thought to himself as he rode into the yard.

Unlike the other stations, there was no horse waiting for him at Ficklin's Springs. Walking the sweating sorrel over to the corral, Sam stripped the bridle from its mouth, loosened the girth to let the horse drink, but kept the saddle on. There was a chance he'd have to keep riding the same horse for another leg. Due to the Indian attack the night before, Sam had already planned at missing the next change at Chimney Rock. He hoped the sorrel wouldn't have to go all the way to Court House Station, but he had ridden smart and knew the sorrel could make it if need be.

After taking care of his horse, Sam ducked his head into the wind and walked toward the station. Reaching the door, Sam opened it without knocking. Stepping out of the wind was like stepping into a different world. Outside, the wind was howling and whipping everything with its ferocity, but inside everything was calm.

Straightaway, Sam's attention went to the cot where he had left Henry. He saw a mass of ragged and tattered blankets heaped upon the limp figure. Instead of seeing the rhythmic rise and fall blankets make when a man sleeps, there was nothing. Everything was still. Too still.

Beside the cot, the hung-over station keeper sat like a watchful nanny on an old-black powder keg. When Sam walked in, the man turned toward him. His blood-shot eyes were glassy, and Sam didn't like the look on his face.

"How is he?" Sam asked anxiously.

The station keeper shook his head. "Not good. He ain't done much but sleep."

Just then, the pile of blankets moved and Henry let out a groan.

"That you, Sam?" came Henry's raspy voice.

"Yeah, Henry, it's me," Sam replied. By now, Sam could see Henry's normally ruddy face was the color of ash.

"Glad you made it."

"Me, too. How you feelin'?"

"Been better. You bring the medicine?" Henry asked.

"Right here," Sam replied as he drew the envelope. "Doctor at Fort Laramie says to give you a little of this powder."

Sam turned his attention to the station keeper, "You have anything you can use to fetch him a drink to chase this down with?"

Still moving slow from the effects of last night's drink, the man shook his head. "Alls I got is plates, some forks, and a few cups."

"Well, I don't imagine he can drink this out of a fork. Why don't you go grab a cup," Sam ordered the man. He wasn't used to ordering around older men, but this man in particular seemed to need it.

Stiffly, the station keeper rose to his feet and grabbed a tarnished tin cup off a peg on the wall and dipped it in a barrel of water outside. Achy from fever, Henry propped himself up to a position where he could take the medicine and drink. After handing the cup to Henry, Sam poured a little of powder into his mouth. Instantly, Henry's face contorted as he swallowed.

"You sure that stuff ain't meant to kill me quicker?" he asked as he handed the cup back after chasing down the powder.

Sam looked at the envelope and then faked surprise. "Shoot, Henry, you're right. I must have grabbed the wrong envelope. Sorry 'bout that."

Although he'd started the banter, Henry waved Sam off irritably. "If I was gonna die, I'da died from the smell of them blankets. When was the last time you aired them out anyways?" he asked the station keeper.

Unable to formulate a response, the man just shrugged his shoulders.

"That's what I thought," Henry complained as he collapsed back down. "Sam, I told him to go catch a brown horse this morning and give him a double shot of grain. You best go get him saddled and head out. He's got a deep bottom, and he'll be a little lively at first. Run him hard the first few miles, and he won't give you no more problems after that."

Just a week ago, Sam would have taken the advice to heart. He'd learned quite a lot since then and didn't figure on taking the advice.

"Thanks, Henry," Sam replied. "See you back at Mud Springs."

After pouring an extra dose of medicine into another cup, Sam left the soddy. The violent wind instantly smashed into him as he stepped outside. Clapping his hand to his hat, he walked over to the sorrel and then headed toward the confines of the stable. Inside was a sleek <u>mealy-mouthed</u> brown. Sam could tell the horse was excited as soon as he walked through the door. Nervously, it pranced, swished its tail, and stomped its feet as Sam switched the saddle. The horse was big, pushy, and Sam knew it would be a handful. In fact, it reminded him of the chestnut he'd roped just a few days ago. Sam thought if he could just get it pointed in the right direction, it would be a horse that could make the double leg with ease.

Once the sorrel he rode in on was unsaddled, Sam turned it out to graze. He then returned to the stable and untied the big brown. Leading it out into the yard, he turned to get mounted. Full of spirit, the big horse refused to stand still as Sam attempted to mount. Instead, it pranced small circles around him as if unwilling to allow him to mount. Grabbing the near rein, Sam pulled the horse's head toward him. Nimbly, he jumped up, stuck a foot in the near stirrup, and swung his other leg over the saddle. The instant he released the rein, the big horse burst down the trail with the ferocity of a mountain lion closing in on an unsuspecting deer.

For the first hundred yards, all Sam could do was hold on and hope the brown kept traveling east.

Vocabulary:
<u>Mealy-mouthed</u> – A dark horse or mule that has a pale color around the mouth.

CHAPTER 22

In his fatigue, Sam felt overpowered by the brown. Horse and rider were at opposite extremes. Sam was fatigued to the point his mind was blurring. The brown was eager, energetic, and bursting with strength for the ride. Its eyes flashed and its ears were pinned as it ran for the simple pleasure of running. Sam knew he would probably need the brown to make a double leg to Court House Station but decided to let it make a hard run the first half-mile before slowly pulling it back. At first, it felt like trying to pull the reins on a waterlogged cottonwood floating down the Missouri River. Try as he might to slow the pace, the brown's momentum carried them further down the road. Eventually though, Sam slowed him to a gallop, and before they had traveled a mile and half, had pulled him to a swinging lope.

Save it, Brownie, Sam thought to himself.

The punishing crosswind battered them as they headed east toward Chimney Rock. Overhead, the sky was turning darker, and it reminded Sam of the color of water when mixed with the last of the campfire ashes. Something was brewing in the heavens, and Sam was headed straight into the heart of it.

Just a few more hours. You just might beat it home, Sam encouraged himself.

Within an hour, Sam was closing the last few hundred yards to the station at Chimney Rock. As expected, he did not see a fresh horse waiting for him. Instead, all he saw was the dejected figure of a man sitting on a crate on the protected north side of the sod station. Sam rightly figured it was the station keeper. Although he wouldn't stop long, Sam decided to stop for a moment and give the brown a chance to drink.

"Any luck getting your horses back?" Sam asked, trying to elevate his voice above the wind.

"You see any horses?" the man shouted back.

"Well, just as soon as I get to Court House Station, I'll see if the station keeper there can send a few your way."

"They'll have to get here quick. We'll have mail coming from California in a day or two."

"I'll let them know. Them Indians haven't bothered you today have they?"

The man shook his head. "No reason to. They done took all the stock."

There was a noticeable warning in his voice when the man shouted, "You can bet they didn't go far, though. Keep that in mind, young feller."

Rather than just sit in the yard and get pummeled by the wind, Sam summoned a remaining seed of strength and mounted the horse to continue his ride.

It was getting on toward the second half of the afternoon when Sam left Chimney Rock. He had thirteen miles to Court House Station, and then twelve more to Mud Springs. Twenty-five miles left. He had no idea how many miles he'd already ridden, but the thought of twenty-five more miles seemed almost as far as all the miles behind him. Just a few days ago, he'd volunteered to make a ride and take the mail. He had wanted to ride, and he had gotten his chance. Now, all he longed for was a chance to rest. As much as he wanted relief, the only thing to do was ride on. The stakes were too high to give up now.

Astride the brown horse, Sam could see Court House Rock looming in the distance. At the base of that rock was the last station before Mud Springs. The sooner he got there, the sooner he could switch out horses and get back to Mud Springs. After making the switch, he knew he could make a fast run to Mud Springs. The brown was traveling comfortably and could probably stand a little faster pace anyway. Just when he was getting ready to push the gait, something in the back of Sam's mind warned him against it. Imagining the luxury of just sitting still once he got to Mud Springs was almost too tempting for Sam, and he yearned to spur the horse a little faster. At the last second, he decided to save the horse on the chance that something might go awry at Court House Station.

By the time an hour passed, Sam had crossed all but the last few miles to the station. The smell of moisture was on the wind. Thankfully, the freshness helped to perk him up a little. From somewhere within the darkening sky, thunder rumbled like a rockslide tumbling down a mountainside. With

Court House Station nearly in sight, he felt the first wet drop of rain fall on his skin. To his dismay, he quickly felt another and soon another. Before long, they were coming steadily. The drops were small but stung when driven by the gusting wind. Clad in only a thin flannel shirt, Sam tried to make himself small on top of the horse and avoid the rain as best as he could. He hadn't gone another mile before the rain began to fall like a dam had broken in the sky. Within seconds, it was pouring in sheets so thick Sam couldn't see but a hundred yards in front of him. Suddenly, lightning cracked overhead and was immediately followed by a deafening clap of thunder. Quickly soaking up the moisture, the dry and dusty road morphed into a slimy and slippery mess. Another streak of lightning exploded above the horse and rider.

With nothing else to do, Sam gritted his teeth, cussed his luck, and braced himself against the wind.

Bow your back! Sam commanded himself.

Suffering, cold, exhausted, and soaking wet, he had reached the breaking point. A flurry of emotion rushed through him. He had less than two miles to go before the last swing station, and he kicked the brown horse into a gallop. Half in control, and half just letting the horse run, Sam was just hoping the horse wouldn't slip on the muddy road. As Sam expected, the brown horse had plenty of bottom left and must have felt invigorated by the rain. Had they met a passerby on the trail, the stampeding pair may have been mistaken for a menacing phantom barreling through the rain, wind, and mud. Through the driving wind, Sam could hear the smacking of the brown's hooves as it stretched, reached, and pounded the ground. The storm had summoned a wild instinct in Sam, and he rode like a raging prairie fire was chasing him. Running on rage, there was nothing that could stop him now.

Rounding a bend in the road, Sam turned to ride straight into the driving wind and rain. Through the haze of the storm, he could see the station buildings. Unexpectedly, something else also caught his attention.

Instead of the motionless picture he had anticipated, Sam saw several figures rushing through the rain. It didn't take Sam but an instant to recognize the riders.

Indians!

The horse thieves must have struck just before the storm hit, and once started, had stayed committed to their theft. Sam knew these men wouldn't stop and wave at the side of the road. They were on the warpath, and Sam was headed straight for them.

Instead of veering to the side, Sam just let the horse have its head. As best as he could see, there were four riders circling the station and one figure lying in the mud. They were riding fast and trying to stampede a small group of frightened horses out of the corral. Standing in the middle of the mess, soaked with rain and covered with mud, the station keeper was fighting to fend them off. In his hand was a raised revolver. Judging by the body lying in the mud, the station keeper must have been a good shot. Figuring the man had, at most, five shots left, Sam doubted he could stand them off for long.

With the blood still running hot in his veins, Sam did the last thing he would have expected from himself. He ducked his head, let out a war cry, and spurred his running horse straight into the melee. Rain pelted him, mud sprayed around him, and another clap of thunder erupted overhead. At his shout, one of the riders turned to face him. Fear leapt into the man's expression before he ran his pony off the road. The three other riders were still circling, unaware of Sam's presence. Reaching down in his belt, Sam withdrew the revolver he had been carrying. McArdle had told him not to use it, but Sam had different plans.

Wild with anger, Sam pointed the revolver in the sky and fired two quick shots in succession. All eyes fixed on him. Through the storm he looked like a charging demon mounted on the devil's horse.

"Yiiiiyiiiiiyiiiii!" Sam shouted as he dashed straight through the center of the assault.

For a brief second, Sam's unexpected arrival had stopped everyone in their tracks. While the attackers tried to assess the change in situation, Sam stampeded right through the middle of the station toward Mud Springs. As he rode out the south end of the station, he was close enough to see one of the attackers' expression go from surprise to anger. In that same moment, the man put heels to his own pony and started in pursuit. Looking over his shoulder, Sam could see the other three falling in line. Just as Sam had hoped, he now had their attention. Their wet ponies were running as if they, too, had a vendetta against the brown horse Sam was riding.

"Keep comin'," Sam spoke to himself as he gently pulled back on the reins. Although wanting to run, the brown horse slowed just a little as they dashed downhill and across Pumpkin Creek. Water sprayed chaotically as flashing hooves broke the surface. In an instant, they were across the creek and heading up the sloping hill on the other side. Sam continued to hold back the brown.

Looking back, he could see the closest rider's savage eyes as the gray pony he was riding gained ground on Sam. The others were gaining as well. Like wolves closing in on an elk before it collapses from fatigue, the warriors closed in for the kill. The lead rider's saturated black hair streamed in the wind behind him. Had it been only a few days earlier, Sam may have been frightened. Now, he felt nothing but confidence. The attackers may have been riding the best ponies they could steal, but he was riding a grain-fed Pony Express horse. With each second, the attackers grew closer and closer. Sensing the time was right, Sam waved the revolver over head, fired another shot into the air, and gave one last shout, "Yiiiyiiii!"

At that moment, Sam released the pressure he had been keeping on the reins and kicked the brown in the sides. Finally getting the release it had wanted, the horse sprang into a full speed run as if it knew its life depended on it. All the energy Sam had been holding back in the first few miles was now released. Still turned in the saddle, Sam saw the lead warrior's expression go from wicked, to confused, to surprised as the brown horse pulled away from them. It was as if his pony was stuck in the mud.

"Ha, ha!" Sam shouted triumphantly. "Catch you on the turnaround!"

Victoriously, Sam turned forward, replaced the revolver in his belt, and careened toward Mud Springs.

CHAPTER 23

Sam had no idea how long he had slept after his return. He knew it had been long, though. Although he had hoped to feel refreshed, he was almost groggier when he woke up than when he had first gone to sleep. The stiffness in his back, legs, and hips was also worse than when he had fallen into the cot. Young and limber, Sam was not used to the feeling of crippling soreness. When he had finally managed to get out of bed, he walked less like an agile Pony Express rider, and more like a crippled old man. While he hadn't fallen off a horse and been drug across the prairie, he sure felt like he had.

Even three days after his legendary ride, some of the soreness persisted when he woke up. He was still a little groggy, but he was feeling more and more himself after some time to rest. Still, he did take a few seconds to twist his body to try and stretch out some of the soreness in his back.

A long way from your heart, he reminded himself as he stiffly made his way to pour his morning coffee.

The coffee was hot and warmed him all the way through. After drinking several large swallows, he refilled his tin cup, grabbed a few slices of bacon from the frying pan, and eased over to the door. Soft light was cascading in, and the pleasant warmth of the early morning sun felt good as Sam leaned against the door jamb. He took another drink and let the warm liquid coat his throat. With his arduous trip fresh in his memory, he appreciated the satisfaction of just being still.

Looking out into the yard, he saw Dan bringing in the stock for the day. McArdle, too, was in the yard shoveling some of yesterday's horse manure out of the corral. The day after coming back, Sam had tried to pitch in with the morning chores, but the boss had insisted he stay inside and rest. Although McArdle himself had grown weak with the fever, he was adamant about the point. After three days, James was moving better, and Sam was glad to see the medicine had relieved some of the pain and ache from the old station keeper.

Sam also spied the big mealy-mouth brown horse coming in with the rest of the bunch. Swishing its tail at a few pesky flies, the horse's muscular body rippled as it trotted in for a taste of oats. Seeing it made Sam recall just how lucky he had been to be riding such a fine horse on the final leg of his ride.

His run. The ride. It seemed to be the only thing people at the station wanted to talk about since he had returned. You'd have thought Sam was a mythical hero the way McArdle recounted the story to travelers who stopped. All the attention had made Sam more than a little uncomfortable.

Normally, he would have exited the building and gone to attend to a chore that needed doing. However, he was still moving slow, and most often he became the target of many questions and more flattery than he enjoyed.

True, he had to acknowledge the ride had been difficult. After tallying things up, McArdle was convinced Sam had ridden over two hundred fifty miles and spent thirty-two continuous hours in the saddle. Although Sam didn't know the particulars, he knew he had been plumb worn out by the time he'd finally ridden into the yard. In his heart, Sam also knew most of the credit ought to go to the horses like the brown in the yard. All along the line they had carried the message with the speed the mission had required. Had it not been for the horses, Sam knew the trip could never have been made.

It had changed how Sam viewed the horses he worked around. He already knew they were useful work animals and would always be used as such to him. Now though, he realized how important it was to work with, and not against, the horses he rode. Some horses on his run had been big, pushy, and needed a stronger hand. Others had been skittish, frightened, and needed more confidence. And others had only needed to know the direction they should travel. The more he had worked against them, the more difficult things had gotten. Sam was now convinced that by working together, man and horse might be able to accomplish anything out West.

A rustling noise from behind him caused Sam to turn around. Luke had woken up, and was now sitting for the first time in days. His face was gaunt beneath his disheveled blonde hair, but the sheen of sweat caused by the fever had finally disappeared. Sam had ridden in just in time. Had he waited another night, the young stock tender would not have made it.

"How you feeling?" Sam asked.

143

For a second Luke only groaned before responding, "Hungry."

"I'll let McArdle know. He said he wanted to make you some porridge when you got up."

Rather than reply, Luke continued to sit there as if waking up required as much strength as he had. He'd come near death, but Sam knew he was headed in the right direction now.

The rest of that morning, Sam lazed around the yard at McArdle's request. He passed the time not doing much of anything but nibbling on some bread, drinking coffee, and talking with Luke until he fell back to sleep. Boredom at the station could be crushing, but Sam wanted to soak it up while he could. Shortly after lunch, Sam heard Dan shout, and he knew his rest was over.

A rider was coming.

Exiting the station, Sam placed his brown hat firmly on his head. He checked his revolver in his belt. Although he didn't figure he would need it, at least he had it. Walking over to the stable, Sam grabbed the reins of the small dun that Dan had saddled for him. The horse appeared to have a sour attitude about the upcoming ride as it fought tormenting flies around its belly. After checking the cinch and making sure everything was ready, Sam turned and faced the rider loping into the yard. Even from a distance, Sam could see it was Ben from the Scott's Bluff station. After reining his horse to a stop, Ben casually stepped off and removed the mochilla before stiffly walking it over to Sam.

"You ain't in much of a hurry," Sam said in jest.

"Tired," Ben replied. "Henry decided he ain't yet fit for riding, so I had to run a double leg. If you ask me, I think he's feelin' more down from that whiskey jug him and that station keeper keep pullin' on than anything else."

Sam laughed and shook his head. That sounded like Henry all right.

"Well, who knows, you might get used to things here at Mud Springs and decide to stay."

"Looks like a nice place," Ben replied looking around. "Being as Zach ain't here to boss and shout, I expect I might decide to do just that."

Reaching for the mochilla, Sam grabbed the pouch and flopped it over the saddle. Stepping into the stirrup, he swung a leg over and was ready to make the run to Julesburg.

"Well," he said looking down at Dan and Ben. "We'll see you boys on the turnaround."

With that, he turned the dun south and loped out of Mud Springs. As the prairie spread out in front of him, he forgot the stiffness and fatigue that had dogged him since his long ride. Once again, he was in the saddle with nothing but open road in front of him. The wind rushing over his face, the cadence of the horse's hooves, and the blur of the grass below caused a fresh excitement to bubble up within him. The dun accelerated up the road, and Sam eased back on the reins just a bit.

"Save a little, boy," he said quietly. "You never know when you're gonna need it."

With blue sky overhead and a good horse beneath him, Sam Payne was back in the saddle again.

THE END

Thanks for taking the time to read, *History of the West with Sam Payne: Pony Boy.* Please take a moment to rate and offer a review on Amazon. Also, be sure to join the newsletter at frontierlife.net for more history adventures!

BE SURE AND CHECK OUT THE ENTIRE HISTORY OF THE WEST SERIES AVAILABLE AT FRONTIERLIFE.NET AND AMAZON.COM.

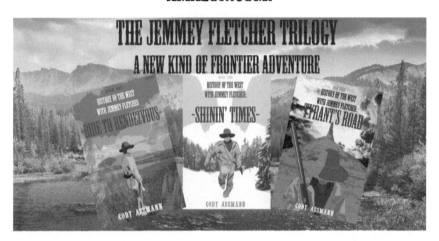